"I GOT TIRED OF WAITING FOR YOU SO I WENT TO BED . . ."

She was stark naked, beautiful, stretched out on Fargo's bed with a welcoming smile. And Fargo had never set eyes on her before.

"What are you doing here?" he asked.

"Do I pass inspection?" she said, watching him look her over.

"I'd give you at least an A-minus," he said casually. "As a picture. But motion is something else, honey."

"Well, how about giving me a chance to raise my score?"

"It might be kind of fun having you convince me," he agreed, starting to undress as he headed for the bed . . .

Exciting Westerns by Jon Sharpe

THE
COMSTOCK
KILLERS

by

Jon Sharpe

Ⓢ
A SIGNET BOOK
NEW AMERICAN LIBRARY
TIMES MIRROR

PUBLISHER'S NOTE

This novel is a work of fiction. Names, characters, places, and incidents either are the product of the author's imagination or are used fictitiously, and any resemblance to actual persons, living or dead, events, or locales is entirely coincidental.

The first chapter of this book appeared in *Border Arrows*, the twenty-second volume in this series.

The Trailsman

Beginnings . . . they bend the tree and they mark
the man. Skye Fargo was born when he was
eighteen. Terror was his midwife, vengeance his
first cry. Killing spawned Skye Fargo, ruthless,
cold-blooded murder. Out of the acrid smoke of
gunpowder still hanging in the air, he rose, cried
out a promise never forgotten.

The Trailsman, they began to call him all
across the West, searcher, scout, hunter, the man
who could see where others only looked, his
skills for hire but not his soul, the man who lived
each day to the fullest, yet trailed each
tomorrow. Skye Fargo, the Trailsman, the seeker
who could take the wildness of a land and the
wanting of a woman and make them his own.

The country around the fantastic Comstock lode, in the 1860s.

1

The tall broad-shouldered man with the lake-blue eyes took in the angry young woman seated beside him in the bounding, pitching Concord stage: raven-colored hair done neatly on top of her head, dark brown eyes in a china-white face, and a soft but now tightly lined mouth; a figure that even under the present difficult conditions he could see was hourglass, with full, high breasts pushing up from the bodice of her trim brown and white traveling dress.

With the sudden roll of the coach, Skye Fargo's arm and shoulder had pressed into the cushion of those proud, provocative breasts, bringing a rush of color into the girl's smooth cheeks.

"Forgive me, miss. Looks like our driver's having a rough time handling this heavy spring rainfall."

"Wells, Fargo gives no thought to their passengers," said the round little man bouncing on his seat across from Fargo and the girl. He was holding a derby hat in his lap. "Company ought to instruct the drivers that us paying passengers are humans and not cattle." He sniffed wetly,

9

fingered the point of his chin. "I do a lot of travel-ing in these back-breakers, and let me tell you folks, a drummer's life is more thorn than rose."

The small middle-aged woman seated beside him, who was trying to hold on to anything she could—except her fellow passenger—turned her sharp nose only far enough toward the drummer to look down it, disdaining a response.

All this brought a sting of amusement to Fargo's eyes as the lurching stage once again pushed him against the lovely black-haired girl. Reluc-tantly he drew back, offering a further apology, though his heart was nowhere in it. The girl flicked her brown, almond-shaped eyes at the ruggedly handsome man, but now the color of her cheeks was a deep red.

"Perhaps some of the passengers need instruc-tion too," she said icily, in response to the drummer's remark. "On how to sit in their own seat!"

Skye Fargo's face split into a big grin at that. His eyes shone as he took in the angry tilt of her head, the concave line of her profile, the tip of her earlobe showing delightfully from beneath the mass of glinting black hair.

"I'm game to take some lessons," he allowed amiably. "Just haven't come across the right teacher—at least not yet," he added.

And at that moment the coach seemed to crash into a small chasm in the road and the girl was flung almost into the big man's lap. Her hair brushed his face and for a fleeting second her hand fell against his leg, brushing his erection which had sprung up instantaneously.

She regained her balance, biting her lip, furiously flushed, keeping her eyes averted and not saying anything.

Fargo's attention dropped to the line of her taut bosom and he realized how really angry she was, saw it in the catch of her breathing. "Pleased to make your acquaintance," he said amiably. And he grinned as she moved elaborately away from him. "Looks like we might be getting close," he went on, lowering the coach window and putting his head out. "It's pretty much stopped raining; just some sprinkles."

"Hyah! Hyah!" came from the driver up on the box. The long black-snake whip cracked out, through-braces creaked, the sweating horses lunged as they raced into the canyon, while the harsh spring wind swept a sudden sheet of hard rain against the stage.

Fargo drew back inside the coach, wiping his face. He was quick enough to catch the girl smothering a laugh.

"Bit damp out there," he said with a friendly grin. "I'm happy to change your mood."

She stared coldly at him.

The drummer put the derby hat on his head, straightened it with the tips of his fingers, touched the spectacles that showed slightly from the breast pocket of his black broadcloth coat. His sharp eyes pointed at the big man seated across from him. "Your name's Fargo, I heard back at Antelope. They call you the Trailsman."

But Fargo had moved again to the window and was leaning out, the expression on his face sour. He had a distinct feeling that something was out of balance, the kind of feeling he knew well on the trail, and which he always trusted. He didn't like the drummer recognizing him. Yet it wasn't just the fact of recognition; he'd been recognized before in his travels. It was something about the drummer.

Had his feeling anything to do with his visiting Virginia City? He was going there in answer to a man named Conrad Rivers, owner of the Six-Mile Mining Company, who had promised him an assignment, guaranteeing adventure and good money. A man couldn't ask for much more, if you threw in a girl or two.

At the same time, he was also interested in the chance of picking up any news of the remaining two of the three men who had murdered his father and mother and younger brother. The search that ran like a red thread through all the minutes of his life; the search that began when he was eighteen and had taken the name Fargo so the killers would not know him until it was too late to escape justice. The vow taken that nothing was ever going to stop him. He had already accounted for one of the three; it was only a matter of time till he found the other two.

The stage had now reached the top of a long, low grade and, pausing for only a moment, started down the other side at full gallop, the driver evidently intent on making good ground over the road ahead. The Concord careened into the valley, the horses scrambling and the huge wheels throwing mud and water. The momentum of the wild descent carried the horses at a gallop halfway up the next slope.

A pencil of brilliant sunlight bore down through churning, slate-colored clouds as the iron tires of the coach rang noisily against the rocky road.

Again the poor footing and heavy drag of the coach slowed them to a walk. Leaning out of the window Fargo looked up at the guard seated on the box beside the driver, saw that he had a blanket over his head to keep off the rain, though it had just stopped. The driver, in a plainsman's leather jacket, looked like he was made of leather himself. He seemed to ignore the weather. Cracking his whip continually, he was working himself and his horses for all he had, evidently in an effort to make up time. His head was bare, his shoulder-length hair soaked to his scalp. His long bony jaws gripped a stubby cold cigar.

The blowing of the horses was loud as escaping steam as Fargo drew back inside the coach.

The little drummer was speaking. "I hear they been having more than a few holdups in this part of the country. Lot of gold and silver moving about. Got to expect it. The Comstock's the Comstock, and it's got to attract the thieves and such."

"Holdups!" The little woman beside him seemed to draw into a knot of trepidation. "Bandits! My word!"

"They call them road agents, ma'am," the drummer said in a bland tone of voice.

Fargo again had that strange sense of something not right. His eyes were on the drummer as the crack of a pistol suddenly rang outside the coach and a hard voice called for the driver to pull up.

The passengers were instantly thrown by the sudden reining of the horses. Fargo saw the drummer's spectacles fly out of his coat pocket, while he himself was thrown toward the girl beside him as the horses made a dash for the shoulder of the road. But Fargo hardly touched her, his bodily reactions so quick that he was off balance only a second. In a flash he had opened the opposite coach door, grabbed the girl by the wrist, and pulled her out onto the bank alongside the road.

Landing easily, he pulled her down behind a pair of boulders from where he had a good view of the arrested stagecoach and the man covering it with a leveled handgun from the other side of the road.

Meanwhile up on the box the driver was sawing leather as hard as he could, the great strands of the master reins coiled into the boot. The panicked horses were brought up on their haunches, half on top of the lead team and with the coach pushing the rumps of the pair of wheel horses.

The guard had pitched forward into the frantic horseflesh. Rolling free unhurt, he threw his hands high in the air.

"Throw out the box!"

It was another voice now, not the man with the gun. The new voice came from another spot along the road, up ahead of where the coach had halted and out of Fargo's view.

He was lying right on top of the girl, who, realizing her position, had started to squirm out from under him.

"Stop it!" he hissed. "Lie still till I see how many there are, and where."

"Get off me!"

"Don't move!" He put his big hand over her mouth, more aware of the soft, mobile body be-

14

neath him, the slight but definite odor of her perfume. "Just be still."

"You get off me!" She almost spat the words, the brown eyes glaring furiously up at him.

"Sorry," he said. "Not a good time for getting to know you." And he pressed his suddenly hard member against her leg.

She had stopped struggling and lay rigid as iron beneath his big body, her legs clamped together, her eyes clenched shut in fury.

He raised himself slightly, moved carefully away, his eyes watching the man with the gun. The other man was still not visible. The man with the gun was tall, wearing a long duster coat and a beaver plug hat.

"Goddammit!" he barked. "Throw out that box! We know it's there."

"Think I'm loco?" snapped the driver as he desperately sawed the reins. "You want them horses to pull this coach plumb over the hill!"

The Trailsman's eyes swept the terrain, then returned to take in detail, first the general picture of what confronted them and then the particulars. Something he couldn't quite put his finger on was nagging him, but he didn't dwell on it. He knew it would come when the moment was appropriate.

They were lying to the far side of the coach, away from the man with the gun. The road was cut around a small knoll. On the east side the hill dropped away gently from the shoulder of the road, but on the west side the road had been blasted through a huge wall of rock. A number of great boulders still lay where they had fallen on that side. It was a good spot for a holdup, for any

15

stage would have to slow to a walk before reaching the boulders, which afforded perfect cover for highwaymen.

Fargo watched the man with the gun motion to the guard. "You get the box."

The guard hurried to obey. He stood on the front wheel and reached into the boot.

"Hurry it!" ordered the voice of the man who was still out of sight.

"It weighs a ton," groaned the guard. But the order had given him extra strength. The box came out of the boot and toppled to the road with a crash.

"Line up the passengers," the same voice ordered.

Fargo lay absolutely still, listening to the girl's breathing. "You stay here," he whispered. "And don't move."

"Where are you going?" Her words speared him—demanding, still angry.

"I've got to find out how many they are, and where."

"But why not just let them have the box?" she said in a hard whisper. "Do you want to get us all killed?"

"That's a dumb question."

"They'll just let us go. All they want is the money."

"No, they won't let us go."

"Why? How do you know they won't?"

"They plan to kill us," he said evenly, and heard the sharp intake of her breath.

"But why? I don't understand."

"It's simple," he said quietly, his eyes still watching the road as he spoke softly to the girl. "The man up there isn't wearing a mask. And so he isn't figuring on any survivor recognizing him."

They were silent as Fargo watched the guard opening the door of the coach, accompanying this action with the quite unnecessary words, "It's a holdup."

The drummer and the little lady with the pointed nose descended to stand next to the guard facing the man with the gun.

Fargo had slipped to a fresh vantage point behind a big clump of sage and now his eyes found the second road agent. The man was standing with a rifle in his hands in the shadow of one of the big boulders.

"You looking for someone?"

Fargo realized the man with the rifle was speaking to one of the three lined up beside the coach; the driver up on the box was still having a time gentling his horses.

It was the drummer who answered, his voice grainy in the wet air. "I was looking for your accomplice," he said. "The big fellow, the one they call the Trailsman. He's disappeared with one of the passengers. That's a neat trick, having a plant right inside the coach." And the drummer coughed out a tight laugh.

"Damn!" Fargo swore as he raised himself to one knee and shot the man with the rifle in the throat. His target had not yet hit the ground before the Trailsman had thrown himself behind a pile of rocks, snapping a second shot at the first bandit, who had fired wildly in his direction and missed. Fargo's next shot was true, the big Colt .45 pumping lead into the bandit's belly and shattering his spine. He collapsed like a red, wet rag.

17

It was over in seconds, the two highwaymen lying prone in death while the driver fought wildly to control his spooked horses and the passengers and guard stared in shock.

"Don't anybody move!" Fargo's words cut hard into the grim tableau as he instantly slipped to a fresh cover, just in case there were others in the holdup.

His eyes covered the terrain carefully. He could see the girl lying where he had left her, the passengers and guard starting to fidget, and the driver finally settling the horses. He waited, looking twice at everything, trying to see in depth, to feel himself into what he was looking at. And he was aware once more of the strange dissatisfaction, the feeling that there was something there that he was not seeing. And then, as he stepped out into full view, he remembered.

"Seems to be just the two of them," he said casually.

"Well you sure surprised me, Trailsman." It was the drummer. "Like you likely heard, I thought you were their accomplice, figured they'd planted you with us passengers for insurance." A pale grin came into the pasty face. "Sure glad I was wrong, and I thank you for saving us."

Fargo's eyes had never left the drummer's face and hands; he noted how small and very white those hands were as he dropped the big Colt back into its holster. His hand dropped to his side, and he started to turn away.

The round little man was fast, the derringer appearing out of nowhere into his small white hand. But the Trailsman had never taken his attention away from the drummer, and he was faster. The Colt was out and up and the drummer was falling it seemed even before the report crashed into the countryside. Fargo had shot him right between the eyes, blowing his head apart.

The girl, who had come up to where Fargo was standing, barely stifled a scream. The little middle-aged woman didn't. She shrieked, and then started to swear; her lips trembled and her whole body shook. She started to babble.

"Handle her," Fargo ordered the girl.

"What did you shoot him for!" The brown eyes stared at the drummer's body in shock and dismay. "Are you crazy! He wasn't doing anything!"

Fargo was reloading the Colt. His voice was calm as he said, "He was looking for the accomplice. Well, he found him."

"What do you mean!" The girl had slipped her arm around the other woman, who was sobbing. "What do you mean?" she repeated. "Maybe you're one of the gang like he said!"

A grim smile touched the corners of the big man's mouth. "They had him planted in the coach; just in case anything went wrong. I was what went wrong, so he tipped them off. You heard him. If you want to turn him over, you'll see the hideout gun he pulled."

"And he'd of sure taken all that loot," the driver cut in from the box, and he released a long, low whistle.

"But how did you know?" the girl asked, her eyes still staring with shock at the swift violence of the three killings. And then her anger moved her toward a stronger control. "You seemed to know it all in advance, damn you!"

"You'll maybe see his glasses on the floor of

the coach were he dropped them," Fargo said mildly.

"Glasses? Spectacles?"

"Except the lenses are tinted blue. Drummers don't wear blue-tinted glasses, but cardsharps do. They use them to spot the marks on the backs of cards. He was also carrying that derringer in a special arm holdout. Anything else you want to know?"

By now the older woman had calmed down and was again rational, though still crying softly. The girl still had her arm around her and seemed to have forgotten her own sense of shock and anger in her concern for her companion. After the two of them had climbed back into the coach, Fargo and the guard loaded the box back into the boot.

The driver released the taut reins. The horses heaved forward, and with a heavy pull he guided them back onto the road. As the teams crested the hill and surged into a gallop, the guard swung up on the rear of the coach and made his way to his place beside the driver. Fargo, who was already atop the swaying coach, leaned down, opening the door below, and easily swung inside, to the amazement of the two female passengers.

There was an expectant crowd waiting for the stage as it drove into Virginia City and pulled up at the Wells, Fargo and Company office.

"We owe you our thanks," the girl said coolly as Fargo opened the door for her.

"Anytime." He grinned. "Might look you up. I plan to be in town a short spell."

Her face was totally without expression as she said, "I don't believe my husband would care for that."

"I wasn't intending to invite him along," Fargo replied easily.

"*I* don't care for it!"

And with her lips pressed together she stepped down from the coach, leaving Fargo with the slight scent of hyacinth and the vision of a superb rear end. His eyes followed her as he moved now to the outside of the crowd, watched her being greeted by a redheaded, sandy-looking man of about thirty. He could only see her back, but he still caught something of her rigidity as she offered her cheek for her escort to kiss. Her husband? Whoever it was, Fargo could clearly see that the girl was not boiling over for him. Maybe he would see her again. The big man with the lake-blue eyes had an idea he definitely would.

2

The letter had been carefully written. Would Mr. Fargo come to Virginia City to discuss a matter of grave moment with Mr. Conrad Rivers, president of the Six-Mile Mining Company? The enterprise would assuredly engage Mr. Fargo's unique talents. Full expenses for the journey were enclosed, and on acceptance of the assignment a handsome fee, a very handsome fee. The handwriting was neat, slightly crabbed, indicating a certain age and avarice, and a sense of order.

At the same time, caution, even secrecy, had been asked for. And so he had left the Ovaro at Antelope Creek stage station and taken the Concord to Virginia City, wanting to avoid the attention the big shiny black-and-white pinto always attracted. Still, he wondered how the little man with the derby hat had spotted him so quickly. Had it been just coincidence? Fargo believed in hunches, but not very much in coincidence.

He had taken a room at a log hotel on F Street, as the letter had suggested, and found a message on his arrival asking that he come to the Ace

And Player on Cohoes Street at eight o'clock in the evening.

He had plenty of time until then and so he decided to see the town. Fargo had always favored picking up background, atmosphere, when contemplating an assignment. Detail and local color were always helpful. And he found this as important in a place like Virginia City as he did on the trail.

For the Trailsman each detail of a place was a sign to be read. But it had first to be seen, not merely looked at. A man's gesture, a woman's tone of voice could be read the same as a footprint in wet ground, an arrowhead, the way a branch was broken or bark on a tree scraped, or the sound or movement of a suddenly winging bird. Everything was there for the man who could see.

He stood now at the corner of B and Territory streets, surveying the ceaseless activity before him. As far as he could see from the north end of B Street to the high ridge that separated Virginia City from Gold Hill, its rival city on the south side of Mt. Davidson, it was one long line of prairie schooners, great drays loaded down with gold and silver ore, huge freight wagons, stagecoaches, and staggering wagons loaded with logs for steam engines and timbers for the mines.

Each log wagon was pulled by a twenty-mule team and trailed by three or four more wagons— back-action trailers—carrying as much as twenty cords of wood at a time. Even the light stagecoaches needed two or three teams of strong horses to get them over the grades.

And it seemed that every mule skinner and

driver had put bells on his animals in order to raise the most vigorous sound possible. The tremendous dust, the seething heat, the odor of sweat and sour clothing, the jingling of the multitudinous bells, the squeal of steel-tired wheels on rock, the braying of the mules and the oaths of the skinners as they cracked their thirty-foot black-snake whips—all brought a reflective smile to the big man's eyes. Yes, the city and town harbored a different kind of danger than the trail, another sort of violence. There was no question with Skye Fargo where his preference lay. Yet he realized that he must know both—the town as well as the trail. For wherever there were men there would be violence. And where there was violence there was inevitably treachery.

He squinted at the lowering sun now in the diamond brilliance of the late-afternoon sky and began walking toward the south end of town, first passing a tent surrounded by men in the center of whom stood a representative recruiting labor for the Black Witch Mine. At another tent a barker was calling for workers on the wood ranches near Lake Tahoe. At a log cabin a tailor had a sign in an unglassed window that stated his need for help. Bars and restaurants had notices calling for cooks, bartenders, waiters. A wagon works wanted a strong man for tightening wagon bolts. A chandler's sign stated that thousands of dollars could be made supplying the mines with candles.

The streets surged with activity, and Fargo wondered if—yes—maybe one of the killers he sought might be here. Everyone was attracted to the Comstock sooner or later. At the corner of B and Holcomb streets he paused in front of a frame house that contained a broker's office. A crowd of speculators was crammed around a big blackboard on which the latest quotes on mine shares were chalked. Money was as plentiful as air and talk in Virginia City. No wonder there was such a rash of holdups.

The building he entered was a two-bit bar instead of a short-bit house—meaning that the drinks were twenty-five cents or two long bits, instead of ten cents or a short bit. He realized that the exclusive price eliminated the riffraff: and indeed, inside the Ace and Player it was as quiet and refined as any place in San Francisco. A finely polished mahogany bar stretched the length of one wall of the room. Behind it a huge mirror created the impression that the room was twice its actual size. There were coal oil lamps with gleaming reflectors on the walls, and there was a gaming room adjoining the saloon proper with a dozen green-baize-topped tables for cards and dice. Maybe twenty men lined the bar, another dozen sat at tables in small groups. He judged them to be brokers, speculators, lawyers, mine superintendents.

"It's on the house," the bartender said as he approached with glass and bottle.

Fargo nodded.

The bartender clicked his lips; he had spilled a drop of whiskey onto the bar. Now he lifted Fargo's glass and with one pass of the bar rag the bar top was dry.

"Appreciate it," Fargo said, reaching for his glass.

"Mr. Rivers will be through that end door to

your left," the bartender said, without raising his eyes and hardly moving his lips as he moved the bar cloth over more of the dark mahogany.

Fargo took a moment, refusing to hurry. Let the big man wait a bit, he decided. He lingered a few more moments, drinking his whiskey slowly.

"Those are the bare facts: I can fill you in on detail as you need it." Conrad Rivers leaned back, crossing his long legs, and with his elbows on the arms of the high-backed swivel chair, made a pyramid of his fingers. His large, cold, creamy gray eyes surveyed the big, broad-shouldered man seated across from him.

Fargo studied the man seated at the big rolltop desk. Conrad Rivers was tall, thin, wiry yet supple in movement, clothed in a well-tailored gray frock coat with matching cravat. His full head of gray hair was striking. He had a high forehead, wide nostrils at the end of a long, sharp nose, his eyes close to the bridge. The voice was soft, modulated, the kind of voice, Fargo decided, that was accustomed to giving orders and counting money.

Fargo was about to say something when he heard a light knock at the door behind him, heard it open as the man at the desk looked up inquiringly.

"I believe you've already met my grandniece." he said, rising.

Fargo had not forgotten the subtle odor of hyacinth as he rose and faced the black-haired girl with the brown, almond-shaped eyes and fantastic figure.

She looked at him without any sign of recognition, her head high as Fargo said, "Yes, we've met. In fact, we spent quite some time together." He watched the color suffuse her cheeks. "But we haven't been formally introduced. I'm Skye Fargo."

"I am Constance Bogardus." Her hand was cool, strong, yet he felt a current coming from her.

Rivers had swept his arm to an extra chair, rising now to bring it for the girl to sit. "Yes, Connie related a good bit of it. It really is terrible the way these holdups continue. The marshal and his men seem quite unable to handle the situation. And I personally am very grateful to you, sir." Rivers allowed a smile to play into his face. "Now then, do you mind if we smoke, Connie?"

"Of course not."

Her uncle reached into the rolltop desk and brought out a box of cigars. "I have these sent all the way from Bond's in San Francisco."

"They ought to be good then," Fargo said as he accepted the offer.

"I asked Connie to join us since she was so close to her grandfather, Jason, and might give you some details that I would have overlooked. And," he added, "Connie also assists me with the mining business."

Fargo had the strong feeling that he was in the presence of a man of consummate cunning. He decided to take the initiative.

"So you want me to find—Uncle Jason." And he added. "Your brother." Saying the words, he watched the other man closely.

There was just a flicker in Rivers' face as he said, "My *half* brother."

"If he is actually still alive," Connie Bogardus

put in. "We had all thought Uncle Jay was dead. Then we heard he was somewhere around this part of the country—up in the mountains somewhere."

"I've already gone into that," Rivers said quickly, cutting her off, and Fargo felt he had stirred something.

He had already known that Jason and Conrad were half and not full brothers, having picked it up that afternoon in town, but he was trying to dislodge some off-guard remarks, gestures, reactions from the cool, enameled pair in front of him.

Turning to the girl, he said, "You call him uncle, yet he's actually your grandfather?"

Under his steady gaze she dropped her eyes. "Everyone called him Uncle Jason."

"How long has he been gone?"

Rivers had been examining his fingernails. Now he dropped his hands, allowed them to fall toward his lap. He took the cigar out of his mouth and said, "Five years. But he was seldom here even before he departed, apparently for good. He was always in and out, and when he finally left the last time we hardly noticed until quite some time had passed."

"How old is he?"

Conrad Rivers shrugged. "All of eighty, I'd say." He glanced at his niece, eyebrows raised. "A good bit older than myself, I must say."

"Uncle Jason should be exactly seventy-five," the girl said.

"How do you reckon that, Connie?"

"The last time I saw him, which was four years ago, he told me he was seventy-one."

"He was undoubtedly lying," Rivers snapped. "But that's of small importance."

Fargo leaned forward. "So you saw him since he left Virginia City."

"Quite by accident."

"Where? Here? Did he come back for a visit?"

"In San Francisco. I ran into him quite by accident," she repeated. "I've no idea what he was doing there, and I didn't realize he'd finally cut off completely from the family. It was a total surprise to see him there. You see, Uncle Jason liked the mountains, the wilds, the desert, Indians and wildlife. He loved all that. Yet here he was at a dinner at William Ralston's. I mean . . . dinner with the president of the Bank of California!"

"Queer," commented Rivers; and to Fargo the man sounded bored.

"It was the most unlikely place, is what I'm trying to say." The girl turned more toward Fargo as she warmed to her story. "Furthermore, he had a most attractive, and quite young lady with him."

Rivers let a snort roll down his long nose. "Jason was always chasing skirts. Daddy told us that often. Don't end up like Jason, he'd say."

Fargo leveled his gaze at the tall man in the swivel chair. "Your father disapproved of your half brother?"

"Indeed he did. As I just said, Jason was always chasing women, drinking heavily, and gambling. The rest of the time he spent roaming around the wilderness."

"Then how do you account for the fact that 'Daddy' Rivers decided to leave all his money to him—and exclusively to him?"

Rivers opened his hands in an offering gesture, shaking his long head slowly from side to side. "I cannot even begin to understand it. It's a mystery. I hope that if and when we find Jason he might be able to explain it. I really would like to know."

"I'd like to ask you one more question," Fargo said.

Rivers nodded, his forehead raised questioningly.

"Jason never communicated with anyone during all that time? I mean, other than the time Constance and he ran into each other in San Francisco?" His eyes turned to the girl, noting how her intake of breath suddenly swelled her bosom under the pale blue shirt, which for a moment seemed about to burst a button or two.

"That was it," she said, her eyes directly on the strong-featured man with the big, capable-looking hands.

"The point is that we must find Jason soon," Rivers cut in. "After all, he's due to inherit a very great deal of money."

"Let me just review it a moment," Fargo said, almost interrupting the other man. "Jason Rivers, age seventy-five, considered an eccentric, left here five years ago, and except for a chance meeting in San Francisco hasn't been heard from since. He is the sole heir to a large fortune and mining operation. . . ." He cut a sharp glance at Rivers.

"Not mining operation," Rivers said. "Jason isn't inheriting the mines."

"Who is?"

"Myself principally, though there are some others in the family. A very few," he added. He leaned forward now to emphasize what he said next. "Fargo, Daddy Rivers left Jason a fortune. It is a *considerable* fortune.

"The Six-Mile, which includes the Ophir, the Red Jacket, and the Quad, he left principally to myself. I don't need to tell you its value; it isn't pertinent to our business here. Now Jason's inheritance will be extremely large; the precise figure is not yet known. But he must be found or the whole thing will be tied up in the courts with the consequent erosion of value." He paused, eyeing Fargo with those creamy eyes. "As I have already told you, we made efforts—myself principally—and also Laura and Kate, my two sisters who are Jason's half sisters. You know we've been trying to verify whether he is alive or dead for nearly six months!"

Fargo stood up, nodded. "Agreed then."

"Agreed." Rivers rose and held out his hand. "There should be fast action, Fargo. I know it's difficult, if not impossible to hurry this sort of thing. But we can't wait much longer; we have to settle the estate one way or another."

Fargo had walked to the door and now turned with his hand on the knob. His eyes moved from Rivers to Constance Bogardus. She had risen and was watching him, her face impassive. But he saw something in her eyes, or felt it rather, a shiver—of hunger—coming from her as she stood beside her great-uncle.

"I just want to know one more thing," Fargo said. "When I find Jason, do you want me to tell him his father is dead and he's inherited all of his money, and let it go at that? Or do you want to tell him the news personally? What I'm saying, Rivers, is do you want me to bring him in?"

"I should prefer actually seeing my—uh, brother—in the flesh," Conrad Rivers said, his soft, firm voice falling like taut velvet into the room.

"And if Jason is dead, who will inherit?"

"I will." Rivers raised his cigar to draw on it. Through the mild cloud of smoke Fargo saw the girl once more. And then he opened the door and was gone.

He had just left the Ace and Player and started along the street when he heard the swift steps behind him. Turning, he found her a little breathless, her nipples pushing into the tight, pale blue blouse, her riding britches so tight along her thighs and buttocks that she seemed to have been poured into them.

"Something on your mind, honey?"

"Mr. Fargo, my name is Constance."

"I know your name; it's your game I'm interested in."

She sighed with irritation, shook her head. "Look. can we talk someplace?"

"Up in my room?"

"For heaven's sake, are you ever serious!"

"About talking with you in my room I'm serious as all hell. It's just down the street there."

"I do not want to go to your room! I want simply to talk to you. Can we take a walk perhaps; we could go down by the Wells, Fargo office; they've a bench there we could sit on. I don't want to excite comment, talking to you, but there seems no place." And she added lamely, "My husband is the jealous type of man."

"Honey, he's got a lot to be jealous about." Fargo's eyes were bright with open admiration.

She ignored the remark.

They had moved alongside each other now and strolled together down the long grade to the little crowd that had collected outside the Wells, Fargo office.

"Let's watch for a moment, may we?"

"I've got all the time in the world, lady, long as your uncle is paying."

"It's fun," she said as the driver came up from the stables with the empty stage and six fresh, eager horses. The crowd had gathered just for this. All watched now as the Wells, Fargo strongbox was lifted into the leather-covered boot just below the driver's seat. They saw the mail sacks stowed into the boot around the box, and then the baggage of the passengers was carried out and crammed into the rear box. What didn't fit there was lashed on top, behind the driver, who remained in his seat, chewing tobacco, too important to engage in menial loading work. Finally four men staggered out of the office carrying a huge iron safe that, with much cursing, they loaded between the seats in the center of the coach.

By now the coach was sagging on its springs. The dozen passengers were looking at it anxiously, but the driver seemed unconcerned. A ticket clerk helped four women to their seats inside and then dexterously stepped aside as the male passengers charged at the remaining space. In an instant the interior was a groping, bulging mass of humanity. Some men still remained without seats and the ticket clerk pointed to the top of the coach, which was already covered with baggage. Finally, an armed guard, holding a shotgun and with a brace of six-shooters at his belt, stepped easily up beside the driver.

"The crowd comes every day to watch it," Constance said at the big man's side.

"I can see why." He grinned. "It's some show."

"Now the fun."

The driver uncoiled his whip, let it dangle clear of the coach, and then blasted it right over the ears of the lead team. The six horses took off in unison. The coach sagged back the whole length of the cradle springs, and then snapped forward as though shot from a rifle barrel. The passengers grabbed hold of anything they could, while the crowd in the street roared.

Fargo chuckled as he and the girl walked away. Turning off the main street, they came to a vacant lot where a tent had burned to the ground the day before. Fargo stopped alongside a bench that had escaped the fire.

"What did you want to talk to me about?"

"I want to go with you," she said. "I want to help you find Uncle Jason."

"Why?"

"I just want to find him. I'm worried about him. Jason—Grandfather—was always very kind to me." A surprisingly soft look entered her eyes. "Funny, we—I never called him Grandfather. He was, as I said, Uncle Jason to all of us, to everyone, even those not in the family." She paused, her eyes inward. "He was a wonderful man. Full of . . ."

"Life?"

"Yes." And she lowered her head, biting her lip.

"Or, are you asking to come along because you want to be with me?" Fargo suddenly speared at her with a big grin. "That it?"

"It is decidedly not!" She glared at him. "You are the most conceited man I have ever met. You are insufferable!"

"Just honest, honey."

"I am being honest with you. Will you let me come along?"

He shook his head. "But don't get me wrong. I'd like you to come along. You need loosening up. And I do believe in mixing business and pleasure—sometimes." He watched her anger rising again, and then said, "This isn't one of the times. It has to be my pleasure too, not just yours."

She stood looking up at him furiously, her swelling breasts pushing outrageously against the blue blouse. "I am talking business, Mr. Fargo. I have not the slightest desire to have anything whatsoever to do with you other than cooperating in finding my grandfather. Is that clear? Is that quite clear?"

"Sure is, ma'am. Only not the way you think. I've got two questions right now. One: why did you come out here and walk me down to the Wells, Fargo office to watch the stage getting loaded?"

Her breath drew in sharply with almost a gasping sound. "I don't know what you mean!"

"Cut the shit. You know damn well what I mean. You wanted to see what, or who, was going into that stage."

She had started to turn away, her eyes darting with anger.

"I didn't tell you my next question," Fargo stabbed at her.

She was hard as a whip as she stood facing

him, the sparks chipping out of her brown eyes. "I can't wait to hear what that might be!"

"I want to know whether you people want to find your uncle Jason so he can inherit his father's fortune; or whether you want to find him so that he can't."

3

The young boy behind the desk looked up eagerly as Fargo shut the glassed front door behind him and started across the hotel lobby.

"You got a visitor, Mr. Fargo." The boy was pale beneath his freckles as he stood leaning with his hands braced against the counter.

Fargo studied the wide space between the boy's two front teeth. "Friend or foe?"

"I'd say friend."

"What did he want? He have a name?"

"It's a she, and she didn't give a name; only wanted to talk to you. I—I'm sorry, Mr. Fargo. I shouldn't of let her upstairs."

"That's right, you shouldn't have."

The boy nervously raised his eyes to the floor above. "She—thing was she was very persuasive and I . . . I dunno . . ." He broke off lamely, his cheeks burning.

"You mean, she's kind of good-looking."

The boy's mouth dropped open. His lips were loose and wet; even so he licked them nervously. His eyes took on a dreamy quality. "Uh-huh . . ."

"Anything else you can tell me?"

"She's alone."

Fargo's hand dropped to the butt of the holstered Colt. "Helluva note," he said as he started toward the stairs. "Conscience never did stand a chance in hell against a hard-on."

In a moment his long stride had crossed the dingy lounge and mounted the stairs. Reaching the floor above, he waited, listening, looking carefully up and down the long corridor. He wondered if it could be Constance Rivers; he'd stopped off for a drink on the way home and she could easily have gotten there ahead of him. He knew she was the type who wouldn't easily take no for an answer and so might likely try him again.

And yet, on the other hand, he was not so sure of any sincerity in her request to accompany him. It just seemed too slick, as though she really had some other motive in coming after him. Why had she wanted to see the stage being loaded? She could easily have managed that without him being along.

The corridor was deserted, silent, shrouded in dust and the gray approach of nightfall. Fargo walked slowly down to his room. Sure enough, there was a strip of light coming from the crack beneath the door.

He waited another moment, his ears keen for the least sound. His big hand closed firmly on the doorknob while with his other he drew the Colt. Then, letting all his breath out slowly, he opened the door and stepped into the room and to one side, standing with his back close against the wall.

The girl was lying in his bed, her bare shoulders and arms outside the covers. She couldn't have been twenty, if that. A kid. Blond, hazel eyes turned up at the corners, a cute, spunky nose. And cool as a spring breeze.

"I'll bet you're Fargo," she said with a smile.

"And I'll bet you tell me your business, honey, in one minute flat or I throw your bare ass right back downstairs into the lobby."

His words didn't faze her one bit. "Why don't you close the door? There's no one here but us."

Fargo had crossed to the window, checked it for possible entry, checked the street below. There was no landing outside, nothing suspicious from the street. He walked back to the door, checked the corridor, kicked the door shut, and locked it. He dropped the Colt down into its holster.

"Talk."

"I'm Melissa Rivers. I got tired of waiting for you so I went to bed."

Fargo stepped over to the side of the bed and, reaching down, whipped back the covers. The girl didn't move a muscle as his eyes covered the young, creamy body with the dark red and rather large nipples, the forest of silky blond hair burgeoning between her lithe legs. His eyes moved along the light down on her legs, swept back up to her navel, and on up to meet the steady gaze of her hazel eyes.

"Do I pass inspection?"

"I'd give you at least an A-minus," he said casually. "As a picture. But motion is something else, honey." He flung the covers back over her. "Now start talking. It isn't hard to figure why that damn fool clerk let you up here."

She sat up suddenly, the covers spilling down around her waist, the pair of luscious, bouncy breasts springing into the room, the nipples harder now, longer.

Fargo allowed himself a moment to admire them, then said coldly. "What's your price, honey?"

"What do you mean?"

"Look, you come whoring up to my room, you've got a price. Somebody sick you onto me—huh?" He reached to the chair that was next to the bed, picked up a handful of her clothes, and tossed them at her. "Get dressed and start talking."

She grabbed the clothes and pulled them beneath the bedcovers, her eyes remaining on his face, taking in the firm jaw, the thick, muscular neck, and the big chest pushing hard against the hickory shirt, then dropping to his belt.

"I guess I'm being crude," she said. "But I've heard of your reputation, Fargo, and I know I can't match the offer Conrad must have made you. On the other hand, he can't match mine." Her eyes moved over his face. "You can't blame a girl for trying, can you?"

"You want me to find Jason Rivers too?"

"That's it."

"Let's start at the beginning."

"Like I said, I'm Melissa. I'm the black sheep of the family."

"I thought Uncle Jason was."

"He's a little older than me, if you like." She started to smile, decided not to. "I'm Connie's cousin. I haven't any money, but I want you to find Uncle Jason."

"That certainly adds up."

"Uncle Jay likes me. He always liked me a lot.

"Enough to give you money?"

"He always did." She looked earnestly at him.

"I'm his second wife's only daughter—we're a big family—and after he disappeared he wrote me that whatever I wanted in the way of money I could have."

"You've still got that letter?"

"Yes, but not with me."

"So Uncle Jason has a lot of money already."

"And he's due to get a whole lot more. The point is, if Conrad gets hold of him I don't stand a chance. He'll pull some rotten deal."

"I see you don't trust Conrad," Fargo said mildly.

"All I could ever trust him for was trying to get me on my back."

"And did he?"

"Only once."

"What about Grady Bogardus?"

"He is my legal guardian."

"What does he do in that capacity?"

"Same as Conrad—if he could. Neither one of those swine would give two bits for me standing up."

"And Uncle Jason?"

"Uncle Jay was a gentleman," she said firmly. And Fargo liked her.

"Meaning he did or he didn't?"

"Meaning he treated me decently." She sat up, but this time holding covers over her breasts as she swung her feet to the floor. Fargo caught a glimpse of two delightful thighs which now she covered.

"Does Conrad know you got that letter from Jason?"

"He does." The glance she turned on him was almost like a child's, he thought. Speculative, wondering perhaps if she could trust him. "I've always been rash. As you can see. I'm very much like Uncle Jay; probably why we always got on so well."

"Outside of the letter, have you had any contact with him since he disappeared?"

"None." She shook her head, holding her clothes in her lap. "When I heard you were coming to meet Conrad—it was a pretty public secret I must say—I decided you were the man to help me. Everyone says you're the best." She paused with a little shrug. "Best tracker, I suppose, hunter, plainsman, scout, and what-have-you. But mainly . . ."

"Mainly what?" he filled when her pause lengthened.

"Mainly honest."

"And you?"

"I'm honest too. I am also moral, whether you may think so or not. A helluva lot of people don't."

"I think you're decidedly moral," Fargo said. "And so am I."

Her hazel eyes moved calmly across his face and she nodded. "Yes."

"You want me to find him; and you'll pay me—what?" he pressed.

"Half of whatever he gives me."

Fargo sighed. "Sounds good; the only trouble is I've already been hired. I've already agreed to find Jason for Conrad and the family. I can't cross them off just like that. Sorry."

She looked nonplussed at that, sitting still beside him, one hand picking at the clothes she was holding in her lap.

"I really am sorry," Fargo said. And he meant it.

"Suppose I could give you some clue as to where you could start looking?"

"I'd be grateful, but I'm still employed by Conrad."

"Fargo, I'm afraid something might have happened to Uncle Jay; or that something will happen when and if he's found."

"Evidence or hunch?"

"I just feel it. I feel it strong."

The big man shrugged. "I know how that can be. But I need facts."

"Look, when you find him, will you let me know? After all, I am a member of the family, the family Conrad says he's representing. Will you let me know and not just tell Conrad exclusively? You didn't make that kind of agreement, did you?"

"I'll turn it over," Fargo said.

"Fargo, I'm playing it straight with you."

"You don't have to convince me," the man with the big shoulders and hands said. He was holding her eyes with his, felt her relaxing and tensing at the same time as her lips softened and parted slightly. And then he said, "But it might help me some if you did convince me."

Her eyes were still holding his as he stood up; they watched hungrily as he began to undress.

Slowly he took off his plainsman's jacket, his shirt, and then his trousers. He felt, saw her eyes moving over his big, muscled shoulders, his big chest, up along the strong neck to the firm jaw and mouth, on up to the lake-blue eyes. Her eyes

43

dropped to his hard, flat belly and down to the big erection, hard, thick, and long, with its big blue head, to the balls hanging beneath, which were obviously filled to overflowing.

He sat down on the edge of the bed and her eyes moved down along his thighs and powerful legs, then hungrily back to the hard, high thing between his legs. Her finger reached up and she touched its wet head, circling the wetness around its edges, under the especially sensitive area of the head. Closing her eyes in rapture, she leaned forward and rubbed it along her face, in her hair, on each of her eyelids, and opened her full wet lips to receive it deep, deep down her eager throat.

She released him with a whimper as he brought his body on top of hers, her legs parting like air to receive his pulsing organ.

"Oh God, Fargo; I want it. I want it. I want you, you, you! Give it to me! Dear God, give it to me! Give me that great big beautiful thing!"

And she reached down to guide him into her swollen, soaking hairy lips; with a gurgling sound he slid slowly, with maddening patience, deep, deep inside her quivering, praying, begging body.

Slowly they stroked together; long, almost to the very end, and not quite slipping out of her.

"Be careful! Be careful!" she begged. "I can't bear to lose it now!"

And then increasing his stroke he rode her with rhythmic ease, faster, deeper, higher, then lower, and returning to a slow stroke until she was begging him to come.

But he didn't. He was bringing her to the edge of the acute impossible, her quivering—and his— divinely in a new tempo as they moved as one, neither taking nor giving alone, but both together in a matchless giving, taking, giving, taking.

Meanwhile his hands played with each saucy breast, caressing, twirling each nipple, then taking each one in his mouth to suck, to nip at, to tantalize with his tickling tongue, until she seemed to go mad, suddenly increasing her stroke, gasping, panting, all but screaming aloud as he rode her into oblivion.

They lay on their backs, panting, wet with the delicious perspiration of their lovemaking.

"My God, Fargo!"

"My God, Melissa!"

Her laughter tinkled across the side of his face. Presently she let her hand run over his face, down to touch his lips, his jaw, down his neck and chest and shoulders. She continued to caress him, raising herself up on one arm to look down at him. "You've sure got muscles."

"I need 'em."

"Especially down there," she said with a giggle, and squeezed his half-rising organ.

Suddenly her fingers went to the half-moon-shaped scar at the top of his forearm. "What's that?"

"A love souvenir from a sweet grizzly."

"Love?"

"I was joking. I wasn't paying attention and he got me. First—and the last time," he added with a wry grin.

"Can I stay awhile?"

"You can stay as long as you like," he said, and he cupped her face in his big hand. "If you like I might even let you make love to me again."

She nestled her face against his big chest. "I

might go along with that." And her fingers crept down his chest and abdomen to touch again his huge maleness.

Fargo spent the following day hanging around town seeing what he could pick up on Jason Rivers. But by sundown he'd discovered little that was fresh. Yes, the name was known; mostly by old-timers. Yes, he was a character, "An old coot who could lie himself off a anthill stakeout, by God!" was how someone put it. An old geezer favoring the firewater, the gambling, and the young girls, Jason was liked, had been a fixture around the town and environs, yet more than just an old trapper, prospector, or mountain man long on stories and short on years to come. Fargo got the definite feeling that Jason Rivers was more than average, he was a good bit special somehow.

"Hell," was the way one old-timer put it, "Hell, he up and told his paw—Daddy Rivers that was—he could go piss up a rope. Heard him say them very words myself in the Silver Dollar one forenoon. You realize, he was tellin' more 'n a billion dollars to go take a piss!"

The old-timer who offered this tidbit spat aimlessly on the dirt floor of the tent bar. "Buffalo-witted, he was! Could've had the Six-Mile and the whole shebang in his pants pocket, and all the girls and booze he wanted from here to breakfast. But old Jason, he had the go-yonders and he told his own paw to by God shove it!"

The grizzled face disappeared into a series of wrinkles as the old man started to chuckle. "Thing was with Jason, see, he always figured he knew more 'n anybody. But not mean like. He just figured he knowed everything, and he by God *knowed* he knowed everything!"

But no one had a notion where the old boy might be.

"Everybody says he was crazy for the mountains," Fargo said to another veteran of the trail.

"That is so, young feller. And good luck to you." The old man looked as though he might be made of hickory as he opened his arms wide, offering the whole of the Great West. "Good luck to you," he repeated. "You find old Jason, you'll be the first man ever located a fart in a windstorm." The hairy face folded into rasping, coughing laughter, mounting swiftly until the old boy had laughed himself into exhaustion, clutching at the bar to keep from total collapse.

It turned out to be Melissa who, perhaps inadvertently, gave him his only lead.

"One thing I liked so much about Uncle Jay was the way he treated his squaw," she said that evening.

They were lying in Fargo's bed and the big man raised up on an elbow and looked down at the girl. "Squaw?"

"His wife. He had an Indian wife. Maybe he still has."

"Was this around here?"

She nodded. "Yellow Wing. I liked her."

"What tribe?"

"I don't know. Maybe Shoshone."

"When did you know her?"

"Oh, maybe six years ago, something like that. I remember how pleased Uncle Jay was the way we got along. The rest of the family was pretty awful to her. This didn't endear them to Uncle Jay."

"How was Constance?"

"Connie's a puritan. I never saw her with Yellow Wing, or even heard her view on the matter. So she probably handled it badly." And then Melissa added, "At least, she plays the puritan."

Fargo caught the edge in her voice.

"But Uncle Jay liked Connie," he pressed.

"He always had a weakness for a pretty face," the girl said sourly.

"I've got the same weakness." Fargo said. He looked down into the sparkling hazel eyes. "I'm sure glad you're no puritan."

"I always figured that for a waste of time."

"You're so right," the big man with the strong, tender hands said as he reached out and touched the side of her face while he rolled over on top of her, and her legs fell open.

He had decided to head back the next morning to Antelope stage station to pick up the Ovaro. But for a moment or two this appeared not so simple. At the Wells, Fargo office he was told the eastbound stages were so filled that it was necessary to book two weeks in advance.

But Conrad Rivers, a man of executive sinew, secured him passage in a matter of half an hour. It was good to get out of town, even though he had to forgo further pleasures with Melissa.

It was still early spring, and with spring had come the Washoe Zephyr, the fury of the wind falling suddenly upon the town of Virginia City, assaulting it simultaneously from the north side of the mountain, from the south, and down from over the top. The ride out of town was swift, the wind speeding them on their way, and now and again almost threatening to capsize the coach.

"Think we'll get held up?" the man hunched next to Fargo on top of the stage said as they rocketed out of town.

"Only one way to find out."

His companion grinned at the terse humor.

They reached Antelope without mishap, Fargo having traveled on full alert the entire way.

He found the pinto in the corral out back of the stage station. The big horse nickered as he came quickly toward him.

The Trailsman grinned. He was beginning to feel human again, he decided. Now as he rode the big horse with the gleaming white midsection and jet-black forequarters and hindquarters away from the station, he gave a great sigh of relief.

He had decided on his course of action, remembering Yellow Wing, remembering how Indians loved to gossip, remembering how life on the plains and in the mountains required no books, no newspapers. In the tribes everyone knew everything that was going on, something the whites didn't fully realize and understand.

Now it would be a question of trust. Fargo had Indian blood in his veins, and it was known by many of the tribes. He hoped the Shoshones would be open to him. It was a long shot, he told himself, but right now it was the only game there was.

He rode at a good pace, not pushing the big

horse, noting the country well as he headed toward the mountains.

It had been a hard winter and the snow had stayed late in the land. Now the ground was softening as the creeks and rivers filled with melting snow and ice, and the cottonwoods along their banks eased into the slow spring, with the good buffalo grass stretching across the prairie.

Presently, as he drew closer to the mountains he saw buffalo cropping the feed, rubbing their great shaggy bodies against the cottonwoods, peeling off the bark as their thick winter coats dropped from them. And then in the tall timber and long valleys lush with meadow grass he watched elk and antelope and blacktail deer. On a high tableland he saw blue grouse, remembered its taste as having no equal among fowl. But he had no time for such pleasures and in the evening was satisfied with stale jerked meat and canned peaches.

At the end of the day he examined his weapons, honing the Arkansas throwing knife on stone and soft leather until it was sharp enough to shave the hair on his leg. His Sharps and his Colt .45 were oiled and in perfect order. He would be ready for close fighting or distance shooting. When the moon rose over the dark land he piled into his bedroll and just before falling asleep thought of Connie Bogardus, wondering just how cold a fish she was. He had a notion she wasn't so cold as she looked, and he asked himself again if maybe she really did want to help him find Jason Rivers.

At dawn he awakened to the song of a purple finch. In the presence of the warming sun he ate a hard dry breakfast and was soon riding east and north, traveling swiftly and quietly below the crests of aspen-covered hills, reading the land, the sky—not only with his eyes and ears, or sense of smell, but with his very skin. The Trailsman understood well that to know the land he had to know it like his own body.

Around the middle of the forenoon he rode to a stream bank and rested the Ovaro. For a while he had been reading signs that told him Standing Eagle's Shoshone camp was not far. Fargo had encountered the chief some years ago; he knew some Shoshone and was skilled in the sign language of the plains tribes. He hoped the chief would remember the time he had helped the Shoshone get back their stolen horses.

While the Ovaro let the cold creek water wash around its legs, Fargo pondered again on the Rivers family. Of the three he had encountered, Conrad seemed the easiest to assess. From the inquiries he'd made around Virginia City, it appeared the man had all the money and power he could possibly need, and that anything added by Daddy Rivers would just be frosting.

On the other hand, it was crystal clear that Melissa was in need. While he knew nothing of her status in the family, he believed her statement that she was the black sheep. She certainly came off as the sort who would delight in shocking the staid and stuffy. As for Constance, she was a mystery. Clearly, her tastes were expensive. Her clothes, her whole attitude spoke of money and privilege. He could easily imagine her leading her husband by the nose. He had discovered that Grady Bogardus was a land speculator who did well, though he wasn't on the same financial level as Conrad. Other relatives who lived in the vicinity were evidently well established financially. There was, then, not the slightest gossip or evidence that the Rivers family, save for Melissa, was in desperate or even mild need of money. He had to assume for the present at least that the search for Jason was on the up-and-up. They really did want to find him so that he could inherit. Otherwise, as Conrad had told him, the courts could tie everything up for years. Of course, it was also a question whether or not Jason was even still living.

But Fargo never finished his thoughts. The sudden crackle of rifle fire, not so very far away, broke across the tranquil meadow and the Ovaro raised his head swiftly from the cool creek water.

From the crest of the long rise of sage, from beneath the wide-brimmed Stetson hat, Skye Fargo swiftly took in the scene in the small stretch of land below. Six very strange-looking wagons were racing across the level ground, the horses stretched out at full gallop, while a screaming band of some twenty Indians rode in hot pursuit, firing rifles and bows and arrows as they narrowed the gap between themselves and their quarry.

All at once a lead horse of the brightly painted forward wagon went down, the other horses piling right on top, and the wagon hurtling over onto its side.

"Prairie-dog hole," Fargo muttered as he watched the wagons that were following pull aside just in time to avoid a mere serious pileup.

The pursuers instantly fanned out to circle the

strange caravan, keeping up a steady fire. Fargo had already kicked the Ovaro into a gallop, racing down the long slope, and in a moment was within range for the big Sharps, which he brought up and fired.

He saw some of the attackers turn in surprise as his target pitched to the ground. Swiftly he drew rein, sighted again, and brought down another Indian. He had the range on them and, seeing the bows and arrows at closer view, realized how few of the attackers had rifles. Moreover, the surprise and accuracy of his attack had cut their momentum.

At a signal from their leader they suddenly turned their ponies and raced away, someone from one of the wagons firing after them, but with no effect. The hostiles vanished over the edge of a draw.

Fargo remained where he was, sitting the Ovaro, reloading the Sharps, as two men on horseback rode out from the little caravan. He studied them as they pushed their horses over the hard ground while he holstered the Sharps and kneed the Ovaro.

"Howdy, sir." The short man's tone was affable, even though he was having difficulty staying in his big box saddle and was bouncing around like a cork. "We are in your debt. sir!" He was wearing an enormous hat and now he touched its incredibly wide brim with two fingers. "I am Dr. Elihu Forepaugh, and my companion is Colonel Clyde Toole." He nodded to the man on the big dappled-gray horse beside him who was dressed in white fringed buckskins, a wide white hat, and gauntlets, also fringed. The man was tall and lean, with a long face, a beaked nose under which a handlebar mustache flowed. From beneath the big white Stetson long curly brown hair spilled to his narrow shoulders.

"Colonel Toole has been guiding us—" the little man started to say, when Fargo cut him off.

"Get back to the wagons, they'll be hitting you again more than likely." And he had already started to trot the big pinto horse toward the caravan.

As he raced in to the wagons with the men and women and a few children climbing down from them, he was shouting orders. "Get the wagons over to that cutbank by the cottonwoods. Pull them into a right angle. We'll try to cross-fire them when they hit again!"

He had pulled up by the front wagon and the buckskinned scout and the man named Forepaugh galloped up to him.

"You mean them red devils is comin' back?" demanded the man in white buckskin.

"They're not sitting out there knitting," snapped Fargo. "Get this outfit over to that cutbank and maybe you can save your ass." He turned the Ovaro. "On the other hand, maybe you can't," he called out as he galloped down the line of already moving wagons to the overturned rig, where some men had already unhitched the horses.

The buckskinned scout's words echoed after him. "We already whipped them red bastards! They ain't comin' back to mess with the likes of us!"

But a man standing beside the downed horse was calling to Fargo. "Leg's broke!"

"Shoot him," Fargo said, circling the spilled wagon, on the side of which was a big sign that said DOCTOR ELIHU FOREPAUGH'S MAGICAL MEDICINE SHOW AND CIRCUS. He caught a glimpse of the other wagons, all but one of which were similarly painted in ornate colors and with carved designs. The exception was a flat wagon with three cages on top; one cage contained some monkeys, the second contained a mountain lion, and the third housed a brown bear. But it was the wagon now taking the lead that was the most extraordinary with its riot of colors, its gold leaf, ornate shell carving, and strips of metal placed as design on the wheels that emitted a loud singing as the driver whipped the team into a gallop and hurried to the cutbank and cottonwoods.

"We'll whip them again, damn them!" called out Elihu Forepaugh as he raced after Fargo. "We'll set their red asses afire!"

Fargo was amazed that he kept his seat as he watched the little man grabbing leather and air. It was when a current of wind shifted that he realized Doc Forepaugh and the "Colonel" were both soused.

Fargo had followed the wagon with the singing wheels right up to the cutbank, ordering the driver to turn the team. Quickly he ordered the other wagons to form an L and for the men and women to make ready for an attack, telling some of them to get out of the wagons and fort up on the ground behind the wheels.

And none too soon, for at that very moment the attacks came screaming up and out of the draw into which they had disappeared it seemed only moments before. They charged right into the wagons, firing rifles and bows and arrows, and swinging tomahawks.

From the side of his eye Fargo saw a woman firing from a window of the lead wagon, while three riders bore in, low on their mounts, one of them shooting from beneath his horse's neck. Fargo brought up the Sharps and cut down a big warrior with a single feather in his hair. The woman in the wagon accounting for another, and Fargo shot the horse of the third Indian, who landed on his feet and was instantly swept up by a companion to sit behind him on his painted pony. The hostiles broke, swung wide, and raced away.

Fargo called out for everyone to check their weapons and ammunition. And in only moments the Indians raced again over the lip of the draw, spreading out like an opening fan, and then narrowing again as they rode right through the caravan. But the defenders, who were clearly unskilled in Indian fighting, held staunchly and on another charge the attackers were unable to run through them.

For the next attack Fargo ordered the circus people to hold their fire until he gave the orders. They were running low on ammunition, and none of them were marksmen.

In the next screaming melee Fargo was again aware of the woman firing from the wagon with the singing wheels. He had a view of her curly brown hair falling to her shoulders, her shirt ripped open revealing the contour of a high, firm bosom, heaving and quivering with the exertion of the battle as she reloaded her rifle. She was smudged with black powder from the Hawkens she was firing. Yet Fargo had a moment to register a high-spirited, earthy, sensuous kind of beauty, and a body that moved with grace. She was young, though not a kid, like Melissa Rivers. She looked like she knew something about herself, he decided in a flash.

Noticing that the Hawkens had jammed, he grabbed up a Henry that had fallen from the grasp of a man who had an arrow through his head and passed it to her.

"We're doing nicely!" she called out from the wagon.

"You're doing pretty damn well," he muttered to himself as he turned his horse toward the wagon with the cages. The animals were screaming and chattering with terror.

And again the enemy was at them. Fargo waited until the very last second before giving the order to fire. Then he saw the flaming arrows—two of them—arcing toward a canvas-topped wagon from which some men were firing at the attackers. Both arrows, alive with flame, found the canvas top, and in an instant the whole wagon had caught, with its occupants pouring out onto the ground.

Suddenly a woman screamed above the uproar. "Carlos!" Turning from the fire, Fargo saw the Indian horseman bearing down on the small, toddling child, his tomahawk raised for the strike.

In a moment Fargo was out of the saddle and fired point-blank at the attacker: the man's head disintegrated in a great splash of blood. The horse galloped on with its headless rider flopping on its back.

But now a second hostile had swung his pony from the charge and was racing toward the child, who was only a few feet from its mother. Fargo had no time to reload as he ran toward the horseman. As the Indian and his pony bore down, he ducked the swinging tomahawk and with a tremendous stroke brought the hard steel barrel of the Sharps against the foreleg of the painted pony.

The animal stumbled, its rider hurtling to the ground. In an instant Fargo was at him, knocking the tomahawk from his hand, his fingers digging into the red man's throat. His opponent had a neck of steel and was trying to gouge Fargo's eyes out. Fargo suddenly went limp, collapsed backward, using his adversary's momentum to roll on his back and, bringing up a fierce kick into the Indian's crotch, hurl him over his head. The Indian landed with a grunt against a wagon wheel, his breath chopping out of him. The Trailsman was on his feet in seconds and with one savage blow against the Indian's biceps paralyzed his arm so that he dropped the wicked-looking knife he had drawn.

The red man had gone to his hands and knees, and now Fargo brought a chopping blow with all his weight behind it onto the man's temple. There was no life in the body that hit the ground.

There was no further attack after they withdrew this time, taking four dead and several wounded with them.

As for the circus people, two men had been killed and two more had received serious, though not mortal, wounds. Others had received minor damage, and to these the women were addressing themselves while Fargo helped the two men. One had been shot in the thigh, just missing the bone, and the other had taken an arrow in his side.

"We sure whipped them Sioux," the colonel said, his face wreathed in a huge smile. "Thank you for yer help, sir!"

"Those weren't Sioux, mister," the Trailsman said, and his words were hard as flint. "They were Bannocks. And they followed you up here into Shoshone country." His eyes were chips of ice as he looked at Forepaugh and the colonel. "Dammit, you could have started a whole war. And you still might!"

4

"The name is Candy."

"Candy? That's real sweet."

"It can be."

"What kind of candy are you?" Fargo asked.

"O'Hara."

"Candy O'Hara, I'm Skye Fargo."

Under the curly brown hair, the green eyes were widely spaced and now moved appraisingly over the broad shoulders and big chest, swung down to the waist, then back up to meet the firm chin above the muscular neck and the calm, lake-blue eyes.

"You dropped by at just the right moment."

"Always try to." He let a grin start to play at the corners of his mouth.

The girl came to his shoulder. In her baggy trousers and her loose, torn shirt, with dark smudges on her face and her unruly hair spilling in every direction, she touched him with a vi-brating, intense animal appeal. Fargo stood still, bathing in the resolute strength of the force that came from her and mixed with his own.

"Nice, ain't it?" she said, biting down gently on her lower lip as her eyes played into his.

"Beats working for a living."

"Playing . . ."

"That is the game. You work for Forepaugh?"

"Forepaugh works for me." The playing was gone. The perceptible hardening in her voice gave him an instant clue to another side of her character.

"You mean you're the boss of this circus?"

"I am. And those two know it." She nodded toward Elihu Forepaugh and the colonel, who were some yards away, deep in discussion over the fight with the Indians. She and Fargo had started to stroll around the campsite while she showed him some of the circus.

"What're you doing this close to Indian territory?" Fargo asked. "You know you can get your hair lifted that way."

"That's what I just found out." She made a gesture with her head toward Doc Forepaugh and Clyde Toole. "We were camped down near a place called Elk Crossing, and since I like to draw pictures now and again I rode out one day to see if I could locate some buffalo. Time I got back the boys there had gotten into a game of three-card monte with some of those Indian visitors we just had."

"I take it the boys slickered them."

"They took everything right down to their breechclouts. Horses, guns, the works." She shook her head in exasperation. "And of course the damn fools sold them some of Forepaugh's mixture."

"What's that?"

"It's the medicine he pitches with the show. It

61

gets you drunk, blind, and crazy all at the same time. 'Course the Indians loved it, and they loved the gambling. They did not love the losing, or the head built for a horse when they began to come round to sobering."

"And your—uh—scout there told you of a short-cut to get away from them."

"That he did." She grinned ruefully. "I guess we got off easy."

"I wouldn't say you'd got off yet."

She stared at him, her eyes large and round. "You mean . . ."

"They could come back."

"Shit!"

"I'd suggest you get moving."

"Sure—sure. But where? That horse's ass, Toole, couldn't guide us out of an empty potato sack."

"I'll draw you a map," Fargo said. "You're not too far from Oro, though myself I'm not too famil-iar with the country."

She was silent as they resumed their walk, while he looked at the animals, talked with some of the circus people. The animals he could see were pretty mangy; the monkeys had tufts of hair missing and they stank while the mountain lion looked as though he hadn't had a square meal for weeks. The bear on the other hand, looked reasonably well fed, and his coat was al-most shiny. There were two moldy parrots, a crow, and a number of snakes.

Candy introduced him to the performers: the Great Cordini, high-wire artiste; a fat man who played the clown; a roping performer named El-bows McFowles, formerly a bronc stomper who, as Candy later said, had had his guts busted and his head scrambled; a big man built like a wagon who went by the name and title of Irish Packy O'Corrigan, heavyweight boxing champion of Ireland and California.

"Packy takes on all comers," Candy said. "If you last a round you get two dollars, two rounds you get four; if you last three rounds you get eight. Like that."

"What if you beat him?" Fargo asked with an amiable smile.

"That don't never happen," the heavyweight champion of Ireland and California said.

"He maybe don't sound so Irish," Doc whispered in an aside to Fargo. "When he speaks. His real name's Pasquale Carrora. He's from Italy."

Fargo grinned at the scowl on the giant's face.

"And," broke in Candy O'Hara, "we put on a good show. Doc calls the turns, peddles his snake oil—excuse me, medicine—the colonel gives out stories about the Great American West." She raised her eyes to heaven as she spoke, and Fargo broke into laughter.

"And this is Aphrodite," Doc said. It was the young woman whose small child Fargo had rescued during the fight with the Bannocks. "Aphrodite will tell your fortune."

Fargo found himself sinking into a pair of onyx-colored eyes and felt the pull in his loins as Aphrodite's full red lips parted to reveal very white teeth and the tip of a pink tongue.

"I thank to you for save Carlos," she said, struggling with the language.

"You're welcome."

"You comes to me I tell fortune. Free!" The gold earrings swung as she turned her head spiritedly, and the many gold bangles on her arms resounded.

"And here are the animals." Candy said, cutting in loudly, quite unable to hide her irritation.

"What do you do with them?" Fargo asked, tearing his eyes from the undulating body of Aphrodite, who with a velvet smile and wickedly gleaming look blew him a tiny kiss as she moved away with a toss of her head.

"The animals are atmosphere," Candy explained, calmer now that Aphrodite had departed. "The kids like to look at them."

"People never saw a bear or snakes before?"

Candy grinned, rubbing her hands together. "They never heard a bear talk or a snake sing. The colonel can throw his voice, see. Makes it seem like the animals." She shrugged. "Hell, it fools some of the kids. People like to be fooled."

"I'd like to take in your show."

"You're welcome." Her expression grew suddenly serious. "Fargo, would you figure on sticking with us till we get out of this mess? I mean, if those Indians come back, or we get lost again with Toole."

"How the hell did you ever get him as a scout in the first place?"

"Forepaugh says he won him in a game of stud. Shit. Same way he lost the circus to me." She grinned at Fargo's appreciative laughter. "Toole was okay when we were just traveling back and forth between Oro and Elk Crossing. But anybody could handle that trip."

"I told you I'd draw you a map," he said.

She stopped walking suddenly and looked up

at him quizzically, a smile playing in her green eyes. "Wish I could talk you into otherwise."

"Talk is for kids."

She was standing very still, the tip of her tongue just touching her upper lip. Fargo again felt the heat coming from her.

"Well, stay for grub; maybe I can work up a better offer."

The sun had just reached the horizon now and Fargo said, "I meant it when I said they could come back. Not right away, on account of this isn't their country and they'll head back to the tribe for help. Might take a day or two. Still, you don't want to dawdle."

"Morning do it?" she asked, cocking her tousled head to one side.

"Might. First thing is to get that wagon up."

Suddenly she stared past him. "What in the hell has he got there?"

Fargo turned to follow her incredulous stare. It was Colonel Clyde Toole and he was carrying what appeared to be a soggy red-and-black cloth.

"It a scalp," Fargo said tersely.

Candy glared at the buckskinned figure. "Clyde, what the hell are you doing with that thing!"

"Figured we'd need it. We run into more Sioux they'll see we're no bunch to mess with."

"You scalped him?"

"I sure did. Slick as a whistle. Learned it from no one other but Jim Bridger himself!"

"If Bridger showed you like that," Fargo cut in, "he must've been dead drunk."

"What are you talking about!"

"You made one hell of a mess of it. You've got to cut all the way around the skull and then snap it off with a twist and a jerk." He made the motion with his hand. "Looks like you sawed it off with a rope."

"That ain't the way Jim showed it."

"Those Bannocks come back it'll not matter what you say Jim Bridger showed you," Fargo said.

"They'll not be back." Clyde Toole said, his voice deep with conviction.

"Not for a while. They know I'm with you and I've got the Sharps," Fargo said. "But they could work themselves up to it."

"You stay for a spell, good sir," Forepaugh suddenly said, coming up to the little group. "I've got a brilliant idea, Candy." He beamed on the girl. "Why not hire Fargo and we can put on an authentic Indian scalping show."

"By God," said Toole. "I can do it. That's right in my line. We don't need him. And I mean no offense, sir," he added hastily. "Why, it'll bring the crowds like flies!"

"Like flies around horseshit!" Candy snorted. And with an angry toss of her head she stomped away.

The two circus men were nonplussed, but Fargo broke into a laugh as he watched the outrageous wiggle of her behind, which even in those baggy trousers seemed to him to be appealingly shaped not to mention energetic.

He had spread his bedroll some distance away from the center of the camp, desiring privacy and also wanting the advantage of mobility should anyone sneak up on the camp proper. But he shortly discovered what he had also known all along: his other reason for bedding down at a good distance from the others.

He was lying on his back naked when he heard the crackle of a dry branch.

"You could've come to the wagon," Candy said.

"I like the great outdoors."

She was wearing a different set of overalls, with the leg bottoms rolled up. She stood for a moment looking down at his big, hard body, with his erection standing in the air. "I see you're dressed for company."

"Take your clothes off and lie down," he said.

"I don't have to be asked twice." And she was removing the overalls, the hickory shirt, and now stood in her bloomers with her high, curved breasts standing out almost as firm as his erection. The nipples were like the ends of fingers, extra long and extra red.

He reached up and, taking the elastic of her bloomers, drew her down to him. She came down on her hands and knees beside him, her eyes sinking into his. Her lips had started to quiver, and now as he pulled off her bloomers a whimper broke from her.

"God, you don't know how I've wanted it."

"With all these men around?" He had pulled the bloomers off her legs and now his hand sank into her soaking fur.

"They're not men."

"They seem to think they are."

"Not my kind."

"What's your kind?"

"Guess." She straddled him, brought her bush right onto his maleness, and began rubbing it gently against the hard pulsing but not letting herself receive it yet. Fargo let her have her way as she rubbed faster, until at last, with a shuddering cry, she sank down and her wet lips opened to sink onto the great stick.

"You're splitting me with it, Fargo. It's bigger'n a gun barrel!"

"And it's just as loaded," he muttered, his face in her hair. He was sucking at her ear and the shuddering went all the way through; he felt it from her as her strokes turned into a circular motion.

Finally he turned her over on her back, drew himself almost all the way out, until she begged him to be careful, her squeals of exquisite agony in his ear, her breath gasping into his face as they thrust at each other, her thighs clutching him, her feet locked together behind his back. Then bringing them down for a firm purchase on his bedroll, she met his long easy strokes with hers, falling instantly into the ecstatic rhythm as they moved more quickly, and her little cries beat against him, her fingers digging into his back, now reaching down to hold his balls, squeezing them to bring the final surge for both as she pumped with him to the soaking climax.

They lay together for a long while, not saying anything, aware only of their bliss.

"I want more," she said. "Fargo, I want more. I'll see you again." And she rose, dressed, and was gone.

Later, when he walked out to check the Ovaro, he found himself facing Irish Packy O'Corrigan.

"I'll get you for this, you sonofabitch." the fighter said.

"Get me for what?"

"You know."

"She your girl? She sure didn't act like it."

"You leave that pistol, and I'll get you."

"Anytime, sonny."

"In the ring," O'Corrigan said. "If you got the guts. In the ring."

"Anytime," Fargo said with wicked ease. "Anytime at all."

Fargo was following a mountainous buffalo path lined with aspen when he sensed it. Immediately he drew rein to study his bearings. He was not familiar with the area, but the signs for danger were the same no matter where you were in nature. He knew he was close to the Shoshone camp. For some while he had been trying to smell it, but the wind wasn't helping and so he was proceeding with special caution when he suddenly felt another presence not far from where he was.

He was instantly wary of ambush, that favorite tactic of the Indians. At the same time he was grateful that it hadn't been the Shoshone who had attacked the circus and medicine-show caravan. Yet he couldn't count on Standing Eagle being friendly. The problem, even when the tribes were at peace with the whites, was the young renegades, young men who wanted to prove their mettle in battle and count coup. Even the strongest chiefs had trouble controlling those feisty warriors.

Fargo sat his horse—listening. The silent heat of the late morning crackled on the mountainside. And the sense of warning grew stronger in him. All at once he turned the Ovaro and rode back down the trail at a gallop. He had decided to use a favorite Indian trick, one he'd learned from the Arapahoes. After three hundred yards or so he cut off the buffalo path and headed for a small summit, hoping to find a spot overlooking a large area. But he was disappointed, for he was able to see no more than a few hundred feet. Still he was positioned so he could brace whoever came along the trail after him.

He listened. He sniffed the air, tasted it. He watched the Ovaro's ears, knowing how much he could learn from the way the animal moved them: the careful listening when they were up and forward, the weariness and sometimes fear when they were down and out to the sides, and the anger when they were laid straight back along the neck. The black-and-white ears were up now and forward as the big horse listened with his rider.

Fargo was wondering what had warned him back on the buffalo path. There were so many things in nature that gave signals: the wren, the bittern, the ground squirrel, the magpie, the chipmunk, the crow. The natural world was full of such friends and a man needed only to learn their ways in order to survive in the wild country.

He had left the caravan the day before, having escorted the wagons to within a short distance of Oroville. It had taken him somewhat out of his way, but he'd had the hunch that were he to simply give them directions, another disaster could very easily strike. While Candy O'Hara was a more than capable bed partner and she seemed quite able to run the circus, he wasn't at all sure that she could handle Indian attack either from the returning Bannocks or possibly from other bands of warriors on the prowl. As for men to help her, Forepaugh and the colonel were no pair to rely on. Of the rest of the caravan people, Irish Packy O'Corrigan seemed the one possible candidate for leadership, save for the fact that all his brains were in his fists. The fighter had not confronted him again; though Fargo had been ready and willing. At any rate, he didn't feel the loss of a day and a half would impair his search for Jason Rivers, and besides, he couldn't argue in any way against the delightful encounters with Candy O'Hara. He sat absolutely still now, listening without the least strain, simply allowing himself to open more to the song of the land all around him.

Then he heard it. The striking of an iron shoe on rock. Just once. Swiftly he dismounted and slipped over to the edge of a short rise. He lay down, and crawled to a spot just behind a large rock. From this position he could see the trail he had just ridden up below him.

He heard it again, the shoe of a horse striking stone. And he had the Colt in his hand. It was no Indian pony making that sound, he knew; it was a shod horse. And it was just the one animal. He was watching through an aperture between two big slices of rock but could still see nothing. Now he heard the horse's hooves steadily on the hard trail and at last the jangle of a bit. Suddenly, just as he felt the rider coming into his line of vision, somebody sneezed. To his astonishment he realized it was a woman. And then he saw her. She was riding a blaze-faced sorrel, and she was alone. He recognized her instantly. It was Melissa Rivers.

"Hold it right there!"

He watched the girl's shoulders jump as his voice struck down at her from above.

"Don't move!"

"I am not moving. What is it you want? I haven't any money."

He saw the rifle in the saddle boot, but she had no sidearm, at least in view.

"Where are you heading?"

"Why don't you come out and talk to me. I'm alone."

But Fargo still had that sense of something warning him.

"That sounds like you, Fargo," she said. He was surprised that she hadn't recognized his voice right off, though he realized now that the only times he had spoken to her had been in his hotel room in bed.

"Walk your horse on up the trail, and when you get around to the top here, dismount."

She was looking up toward the direction of his voice. "Nobody's with me. I'm quite alone. I want to help you find my uncle." He didn't answer and she said, "Thank God I found you."

She had started up the bend in the trail now and in a moment would be on the rise of ground with him. All at once Fargo heard the wren, saw it sweep low in the sky, back down the trail from the direction the girl had come. She was up on the rise now and he signaled her to stay out of sight, hoping that whoever it was had not heard them talking.

When the rider came into view, Melissa had dismounted and crossed to where Fargo was crouched by the big rocks.

"Who is he?" he whispered.

She was bending beside him, craning to see, and her hair brushed his face. "I don't know. I've never seen him before. He just looks like some cowboy or something."

"He is not just some cowboy or something," Fargo replied. "Not with that tied-down Navy Colt on his hip." She started to say something but his fingers swept to her lips and she was silent.

The rider was right in Fargo's gun sight when the big man spoke. "I've got you right in my sights, mister. Don't make a move." The hand that had started toward the six-gun froze. The horse, a big bay, started to spook at something or other, but the rider controlled him angrily. "You alone?"

"I am alone. What the hell is this, a holdup?"

"What are you doing here?"

"Looking for a place to take a leak, for Chrissake!"

Fargo pulled back the hammer of the .45. "I'm not going to ask you again, mister."

He watched the sweat appear on the man's clean-shaven lip at the sound. "You were following the girl. And listen, if you're not alone, consider yourself dying slowly with a .45 slug in your guts."

The rider was lean, with a scar down the right side of his face; his shirt was tight on his bony body. He wore a dusty black Stetson hat with two holes in it, one in the crown, the other in the brim.

"I was following her," he admitted in a coarse voice, the words tight against angry lips. "But I wasn't doing her no harm. Just trying to see she was all right riding out alone like that."

"Who sent you?"

The moment's hesitation told Fargo plenty. "Man I work for."

"Mulligan?"

"That's right."

"You're lying. You got ten seconds to tell it."

"Bogardus. Her guardian, he was worried over her. Sent me along to keep an eye."

"You can turn your horse around and cut out right now." The Trailsman chipped out the words to the man below. And then he added, "And you can tell Bogardus and Rivers not to send anyone else to check up on me or they can shove this job. You got that?"

"I got it."

He watched the lean scar-faced man turn his pony and trot back down the trail.

Later the girl asked, "How did you know he was following you and not me, Fargo?"

"Why would he be following you? You told me Rivers and Bogardus didn't give a damn for you. I suppose you could say I could smell him. And why didn't he ask to see you, see if you were all right?"

She grinned up at him, smoothing her riding skirt with the palms of her hands, her breasts swelling against the tight lemon-colored blouse. "I told you Conrad wasn't a man to trust."

"Honey. I knew that kind of thing by the time I was five years old." He lifted his head, studying the sky. A flock of wild geese swung high overhead, the late sunlight brilliant on their wings.

"That was cute," she said. "The way you figured him."

He looked down into her face, the blue eyes suddenly like quartz. "Honey, if I find out that Conrad or Grady Bogardus sent you after me to check up, you'll wish you'd ridden back with that damn fool." He watched it hit her, her charm dropping before his hardness.

"You're quite wrong, you've no right to—"

But he cut her off fast. "Get your ass back in that saddle. We've got some riding to do."

"Where?"

"Back to town for you; but first I've got a social call to make. Then I'm dumping you."

"Dumping me!" Her mouth fell open, her eyes widened, and he thought he saw them tearing.

"You're in my way. I don't want you slowing me down."

"You really want me to leave?" And there was the charm and heat once again. God, he thought, she turned it on and off like striking a lucifer.

"That is what I just said."

"Please. I won't be in your way. I promise."

"I said no."

"You bastard, Fargo!"

"Maybe. Maybe, honey. But not a *dumb* bastard."

The camp on Horsehead Creek was well hidden. The Trailsman heard it, smelled it before he saw it: a grazing bell sounding from the Shoshone pony herd, the inevitable Indian camp dogs barking, and the smell of cookfires. He rode carefully, fully aware that he was being watched. Crossing the clearing outside the deep stand of willows and box elders, the grass whispered against the Ovaro's feet.

He had left the girl more than an hour's ride south of the camp, high up from the trail in a little box canyon, well protected from any approaching rider. It was an uneasy parting, Fargo having extracted from her a very reluctant promise to stay where she was until his return, when he would take her down to Oroville.

Now, riding across Horsehead Creek, with the shallow water just over the Ovaro's hooves, he saw the tops of the first lodge poles and remarked the unusual lack of movement around the camp. He wondered if the young men were out hunting, for it was spring, the time of year when a young brave craved action.

As he rode up the slight incline of bank on the other side of the creek three warriors carrying rifles appeared on foot.

"I have come to talk with Standing Eagle," Fargo said, speaking Shoshone and also signing with his hands. To his left he noted a thin ribbon of smoke rising from the smoke hole of one of the lodges.

The tallest of the three Indians indicated that he should dismount and come with them on foot. A second Indian stepped forward and accepted the reins from Fargo.

The Shoshone chief was waiting for him outside his lodge, from which an American flag hung limply in the waning light of late afternoon. He was seated cross-legged on a blanket. In his hair was a single feather.

Fargo laid his gifts of sugar and tobacco on the

edge of the blanket. "It is good to see you again, Standing Eagle."

The chief was looking at him calmly. "Welcome, friend Fargo."

Fargo had thought they would talk there and was prepared to sit down when Standing Eagle rose in one flowing movement and picked up his blanket. He was wearing a fringed buckskin tunic and leggings in which little pieces of metal were sewn. Now, as he turned, the late sun and a light wind that had arisen combined to throw little shadows while the metal pieces tinkled.

The chief was a man of more than sixty years and yet he moved like a young man as he stepped to the flap of his lodge, raised it, and bent down to enter.

Inside there were three older warriors, headmen of the tribe. They were seated in a semicircle facing toward the place where Standing Eagle now seated himself. There was one place remaining, at the chief's right, which Fargo knew was for him.

The Shoshone chief was not a tall man, but his bearing was such that he gave the appearance of height, even when seated. There wasn't an ounce of unnecessary weight on his body. And Fargo could feel the quiet strength contained in him as he sat absolutely still, a man well aware of himself.

Several moments passed while the chief prepared the pipe, offered it, and passed it. As Fargo watched he remembered other times he'd witnessed the simple ceremony, each movement having to be performed a certain way, with nothing changed. It had always pleased him to see the way certain of the older Indians like Standing Eagle moved. Even the simplest gestures seemed somehow quite different from those of the younger men. With the older, more mature warriors, there was no waste, but rather a sort of contained fluidity, a precision that reminded him of dancers.

It was not unlike the way the Trailsman himself moved, and his Cherokee heritage was apparent to those Indians who had dealt with him. He too moved as though his was a finer, subtler body than men usually possessed. Yet the Trailsman realized that this observation could only be made by those who knew how to see. To the average man who merely looked, there was nothing special—only a measured silence, or on the contrary, sometimes a blinding speed.

Now in silence they smoked, passing the pipe, and when they were finished, Standing Eagle cleaned out the bowl and returned the pipe to the pouch lined with rabbit fur.

"I have come to ask your help, Standing Eagle," Fargo began in his mixture of Shoshone and sign language.

"I hear you," the chief said.

"It is about a white man and his wife; one of the Shoshone people, one of your tribe."

"You are speaking of Flying Arrow."

"The man named Jason and the woman Yellow Wing."

"The man is known as Flying Arrow; it is the name given to him. He is a blood brother."

Fargo saw the three headmen nodding in agreement with the chief's words.

"Is he here? Can I talk with him? I come to

him in peace as I have come to you and your people."

"He is not here."

"Where then?"

"I do not know. It is long since Flying Arrow was among us. He used to come often, and he lived with us as well."

"Heya," said one of the headmen. "He had young eyes, and a young heart."

"But he went away?" Fargo pressed.

"He went away, more than seven moons past."

"And Yellow Wing?"

"She is not here," the chief answered.

"But do you know where Flying Arrow went?" Fargo felt there was more to it than the words the chief was speaking. He had the feeling that the Indian was telling him something in the Indian way—that is, without actually saying it in so many words.

"Much snow has fallen on the shoulders since Flying Arrow went to the north. It was at the time of the big hunt down in Papoose Basin that he was last with us." The chief paused, searching within.

Fargo tried again. "And Yellow Wing? Is she with him?"

Standing Eagle did not answer. The four faces of the Indians were totally without expression. But they remained silent. He realized they were deep inside themselves as he watched them for some moments.

Standing Eagle was like stone; not a muscle moved; he hardly seemed to be breathing. His eyes were open but Fargo saw they were not looking at anything within the lodge but in some distant place. Then he understood what the chief had been saying to him. Yellow Wing was dead, and Jason had gone away.

A long moment passed. Fargo let himself rest in the strong peacefulness mixed with sorrow in the chief's lodge.

Presently, at a simple gesture from Standing Eagle, the three elders rose and left the lodge. The chief turned toward his visitor. He seemed to be studying him; Fargo realized he was feeling him with his eyes, and now as the chief spoke he could actually feel the words coming from him. Standing Eagle's body was motionless, his voice seeming to blend with the silence rather than disrupting it.

"I do not know where Flying Arrow has gone. He went away in sorrow. Flying Arrow is a man who lived within his heart. And his heart was broken."

Fargo felt again the chief's own sorrow, so very strong because there was not a drop of self-pity in it.

Again the strange silence fell upon them, and at last the Shoshone rose to his feet. Fargo stood beside him. When they went outside of the lodge, a warrior approached leading the Ovaro. Again, a slight wind rose, stirring the shadows thrown by the chief's fringed buckskin in the late sunlight. Fargo listened to the soft tinkle of metal pieces in the sleeves of the tunic. In the light of the dying sun he thought of Yellow Wing.

It was when he was up on the Ovaro that Standing Eagle said, "There are other men looking for Flying Arrow."

"They came here?"

"They asked at the trading post on Piney Creek."

"Did they find anything?" Fargo asked, leaning down from his saddle in emphasis.

"I do not know."

Fargo's brow creased. He took off his big hat and resettled it on his head. "Who were they?"

"I was told it was the gray men, the ones the whites call outlaw." He looked past the man on the horse, his eyes sweeping the softer sky. "They did not ask about Yellow Wing."

"You can trust me, Standing Eagle. I will be careful in my search."

The Indian's dark brown eyes came right in line with the lake-blue eyes of the Trailsman. "The only man to be trusted." he said, "is the man who is not afraid. And so I trust you, friend Fargo."

The Shoshone chief waited a moment and then spoke, still looking into Fargo's eyes, the words coming from some place deep inside. In their softness Fargo heard a great strength.

"Once, many snows ago, you found my horses. Now I wish you well to find Flying Arrow and Singing Flower."

"Singing Flower?"

"The daughter of Yellow Wing. She is still a maiden, and Flying Arrow will care for her. But tell him her grandfather longs to set his eyes on her again."

As Fargo rode away, his thoughts buzzing with all that had come out of the meeting, he could feel the chief's eyes on him, watching him go. As the light faded into the evening sky and shadows penetrated through the Indian camp, he didn't look back. But he knew that Standing Eagle was still there.

He knew too that he had better find Uncle Jason and Singing Flower before someone else did.

The stars were shimmering all over the sky as Fargo rode up the long draw and into the little box canyon where he had left the girl. After hearing what Standing Eagle had said about others who had inquired for Jason, he was glad he had exercised extra caution with Melissa. He wasn't at all sure that whoever had been asking about Jason Rivers at the Piney Creek trading post wasn't also looking for himself or the girl—as the scar-faced rider had been. It was becoming clear that he was being set up not to find Jason and bring him in, but to lead someone to the target.

He had dismounted a short distance from the campsite in the box canyon and had picketed the Ovaro, then scouted the area, taking plenty of time. Only when he was convinced that the girl was there alone and had received no visitors during his absence did he finally slip into the camp.

The moon had risen, and as he approached he could see her clearly seated on her bedroll. Her soft cry of surprise validated the silence of his return; he was almost right next to her before she noticed him.

"You make a hell of a lookout," he speared at her. "You could have been raped, scalped, and staked out by half the Bannock nation before you'd even know someone was saying how-de-do."

She looked crestfallen and defiant in turn.

"There I thought I'd been doing right well." He noted that she had kept the Remington he'd left her within inches of her hand. "I'd begun to worry that you'd left me."

"That I'd left you, huh?" He looked at the tension in her shoulders. "Not worried that something might've happened to old Fargo?"

He saw the smile slip into her face at his bantering—which was what he wanted. She was loose now, and the tight, frozen look in her eyes was gone.

"You've got to keep loose out here," he said. "Sharp and attentive, for sure, but that means loose, not tight. When you're tight you can't move fast, you can't see or hear, and you for sure can't think."

She was nodding eagerly at his words.

"No visitors, huh?"

"None. Although there were moments I thought there were. Guess I was scared."

And he thought she looked adorable as her wide eyes looked directly at him. "You should be scared," he insisted. "If you're not scared at the right moment, then you'll be in real trouble."

They sat silently under the great star-filled sky. Fargo was listening to the sounds all around, reading them, listening for anything that might suddenly strike a different note. It was what he always did on the trail. Everything was there to be read if you knew how to listen and look.

At the same time he could hear her slightly labored breathing. It was less agitated than when he had first walked into the camp, but she was still not totally at ease.

"Tell me about Uncle Jason," he said easily. "What was he like?"

He saw the profile of her smile as she looked down at her hands. "He was really a fine human being."

"And his wife?"

"Yellow Wing was always very quiet. Always very sweet, always there for him. You realize he was a good bit older."

"Did they have any children?" he brought out carefully, watching her for any reaction.

But she was innocent as far as he could tell. "No. He was too old to have children. I mean . . ." and in the pause she gave a little laugh. "He was still able to do it."

Fargo chuckled. "I know what you mean. Kids are hard work sometimes."

"Do you have any idea where Uncle Jay might be, Fargo?" He had been listening carefully for anything extra in her voice as she spoke about Jason, but there was nothing.

"I don't know. I would guess he'd be with Yellow Wing. But where, I couldn't even guess."

"I don't know where you went when you left me here, but I thought you might have had some lead."

He didn't answer, and then after a moment he said, "What did Jason do with himself? I mean, did he like anything special? I know he liked girls and booze and the good life, and also the lonely life, the mountains, living with some of the tribes."

"Funny mixture, isn't it?" And she tossed her head; his eyes caught the superb outline of her breasts and then the intake of her breath.

"I like it all too," Fargo said simply. "Your uncle sounds like he was just full of life, and a lot of people can't take that, you know. Somebody free like that makes them unhappy."

She nodded at his words. "Well, he was sort of all over the place. And he never was much for finishing things."

"What do you mean?"

"Nothing really, just that he'd settle down to something, or so it seemed—and a lot of what I'm telling you is hearsay—but then he'd be off again."

"Out into the mountains."

"Out looking for another strike."

Fargo stared at her. He had the distinct feeling he was missing something. "What do you mean, another strike?"

"I mean like the Six-Mile. He always said the fun was in finding it. He didn't want the digging and mining and all that. He wanted to make the strike!"

"But I thought his father found the Six-Mile!"

She was shaking her head. "That's what a lot of people think, because Daddy was the one who ran everything."

"You're telling me it was Jason who struck the Six-Mile?" He grinned suddenly. "No wonder—then that could explain why his daddy left him all his money. Huh—except it doesn't really; on account of you'd think the old man would have left him the mine." He paused, studying it. "Funny, Rivers never told me any of that."

"Conrad wouldn't tell you anything if he thought it was going to cost him a penny."

"So Jason was still looking for another strike, and for all we know that's what he may be doing right now." Fargo looked thoughtfully at the girl. And then he added. "Or he may not. Funny—once you turn to prospecting, there isn't much else." He stood up. "I'm just going to check the horses," he said. He wanted to think. Suddenly the whole picture had changed. And he found one idea paramount. Prospectors—even the hardiest—sooner or later had to come in for supplies.

Melissa was seated just as he had left her when he returned a few minutes later.

"I'll be taking you to Oroville," he said.

"Oroville? Why Oroville?" There was surprise and hurt in her voice.

"Nearest town. I don't know what's there, but I know you can get back to Virginia City all right."

"There's nothing there." Melissa's surprise was still in her voice. She turned toward him, her face tight with agitation.

"Nothing?" He was thinking of Candy O'Hara and the medicine show heading toward Oro.

"That's where the mines are. The Six-Mile mostly, and some of the others. But that's all."

"Nothing but holes in the ground?"

"That's right."

"People?"

"Darn few."

The big man's brow knitted in thought. What the hell was that medicine show doing there with not enough people to pay them for a day's work, it would seem.

The girl had drawn up her legs and was hugging them with her arms, her chin on top of her knees. Suddenly she sighed, and the nearness of her became more evident as she seemed to release something. Fargo could feel the vibrations coming from the side of her leg, her face, her whole body as she turned to look at him. It was as real as a physical touch even though they had not touched each other.

"But why?" she burst out. "Why can't I stay and help you find Uncle Jay, dammit! Fargo!"

"You'd be in the way," he said roughly. "I told you already."

He could feel her breath on his eyes and mouth as she looked at him, her eyes unblinking. "That's what I want—exactly," she said, "to be in your way." And she reached up and touched his neck just where it met the hair on his chest.

He didn't move, although the heat in his loins intensified as his member started to stretch his trousers.

"Fargo . . ."

"I said no."

"I could be a bitch. . . ."

"Could be?"

"I could be a bitch and simply say to you that unless you let me come along I won't—"

But her sentence was never finished as he closed her mouth with his and, reaching up, began unbuttoning her blouse.

They ate a dry breakfast and washed it down with warm water from their canteens. It was already hot as they mounted up. They rode without speaking through the stinging heat of the bright morning. He was pleased at the way she rode. She knew what she was doing. At the same time, he more than appreciated the way the perspiration of her body caused her yellow blouse to cling to the contours of her delicious figure.

At noon they stopped to rest the horses and bathe in a racing stream. The water was gaspingly cold, and both returned to the creek bank refreshed and exhilarated. They lay naked under the soughing branches of willow trees, the sunlight dappling shadows of leaves on their gleaming bodies.

"Let's not go back at all, Fargo."

"If you never go back, then how can you ever leave?" he said mildly, his eyes running over her prone body.

Turning her head to him, she grinned. "All right, then, we'll go back for an hour and then leave." Her voice faded away as her glance dropped to his enormous erection. He was lying on his back and now she leaned over and with the tips of her fingers brought his member to her quivering lips.

"Time to mount up," he said as she threw her leg across his hard, lean body and slid her soaking orifice onto his great stick.

There was no sound from either of them for some moments save the wet slapping of their bodies, the soaking succulence of their thrashing as he turned her over on her back and rode her to the exquisite climax.

The sun was riding down the sky as they left the creek. As they rode in silence through the late afternoon Fargo tried to put the pieces together. Was Jason even in the country? Had he gone back to San Francisco? Or had he just gotten gaga the way some old prospectors and trappers did, looking for another Big Strike, talking to himself, wandering around half in a daze, dreaming. Or again, he could be just sitting pretty someplace.

Hell, it was easy enough to hide out in that wild country, with only closemouthed trappers, silent Indians, and wild animals to know you were there. And so he was back where he started. Jason had either died, was hiding out somewhere, was a captive of some tribe or other, or was just wandering around, crazy as a coot. But if he was at all rational and free to move about, he would have to have contact sooner or later with some civilization. And Fargo remembered Standing Eagle saying that there had been inquiries at Piney Creek.

It was the moment when the sun's rays were stretched all the way across the land that the trail they were following took a sharp turn and Fargo suddenly jerked back the reins on the pinto. Melissa almost collided with him from the rear, pulled her little sorrel horse back. She was about to speak when he held his hand out toward her face with his fingers wide open.

He motioned with his head for her to look past him. A long line of copper-colored riders was crossing the open plain not very far away.

Fargo drew the Ovaro back into the shadow of a cutbank. The late sun was brilliant on those bronze burnished bodies. Melissa kneed her horse alongside the big pinto as the Indians came closer.

A young warrior led the line, wearing only a breechclout and carrying a rifle. He sat his horse proudly, straight but not rigid. There was a regal quality about him that told Fargo he was a capable warrior.

"Who are they?" Melissa said, speaking softly but with urgency.

"They're someone we don't want to meet," he told her, not taking his eyes from the riders. "Too far away to be sure what tribe. Maybe Sioux, or maybe Bannock. I'd say they've probably got Henrys and maybe a Hawkens or so there. Hard to tell, but forty armed whatever-they-are are no one to play with."

"I counted twenty," she said, her brow furrowed.

Fargo nodded off to their left. "There's another twenty, give or take, yonder," he said. "They'll be meeting up pretty directly. Might just be a hunting party, but we don't want to chance it."

"Do you think Uncle Jay might be living with one of the tribes?" Melissa suddenly asked. "After all, his wife is Indian."

The big man shrugged lightly, his eyes intent on the two columns of Indians. "Could be. But we won't be asking those boys. We'll just cut up over the rim rocks above us. It'll be rough going, but we can avoid meeting that bunch."

Again they rode in silence, mounting the stiff trail, while the sun's rays, leaving the land below to the coming nightfall, shone brilliant on the great slices of rim rock as they traveled higher and higher through stubs of broken and blasted spruce and fir. The sunlight was so piercing now in its final moments that Fargo could almost hear it.

As he looked now at the dead, broken trees he thought of the storm that had wreaked the destruction and pondered on the great laws of nature that in a split second could overwhelm a man and change the course of his fate.

They rode into the dusk, the gray stalk of nightfall following them up to the rim rocks. When the sharp sickle moon entered the sky they camped.

"Are they following us?" she asked, and he realized how scared she must have been, though she'd held back the question during the whole ride up over the rim rocks.

"No, I don't think so. I don't think they spotted us."

He saw how his words were just what she'd been wanting. A breeze stirred and the smell of pine and spruce was strong.

"Fargo, I can't wait any longer," she said, slipping closer to him. As always he felt the animal heat of her hungry body.

"You're going to have to, honey."

"Why? What do you mean?"

"I need to stay awake tonight."

"I don't understand."

He was silent a moment, listening again. "Somebody has been trying to cut our trail," he said.

"You mean—follow us? But I thought you said . . ."

"It's not Indians."

"But who then?"

"Whites. I don't know who."

"But how can you tell?" She stared at him, her eyes wide with surprise, her breath coming quickly.

"Spotted their dust on our back trail a while before we ran into that Indian bunch."

"Are you sure they're following us?"

"You can bet on it, but they weren't sure where

we were. In any case that's one of the reasons I came up here over the rim rocks. It'll be tough tracking us."

"But how do you know they're whites and not Indians?"

"I could tell by the dust they were kicking up. Anyone able to track wouldn't raise that amount, and they certainly wouldn't keep losing our trail." He paused, running his finger along his big jaw. "Anyhow, just in case, I'd prefer being awake should any visitor decide to drop in during the middle of the night."

"But Fargo . . ."

"Pack it in, honey." He stood up and moved away from her, spread his bedroll several yards outside the little circle of their dry camp.

He lay awhile on his bedroll waiting for the girl to fall asleep. When he was satisfied that her breathing was deep enough, he got up and scouted the entire area around the camp. It took awhile, but he didn't return until he had satisfied himself that no pursuers were near.

Only then did he close his eyes and doze; sleeping that half sleep he was so accustomed to on the trail. In this manner he rested, but was also alert to any sound or movement that could bring danger. So he passed the night and when dawn came he had a notion.

He rose quickly, saddled the Ovaro, and rode back down the trail before the girl was awake. It was near the place where they'd seen the Indians that he found what he was looking for.

The hoof prints were clear in the dusty trail, and in the broken stems of grass, the sod was churned by iron shoes, the way no Indian pony would have done. Four horsemen. They had lost the trail again and had ridden out onto the plain that the Indians had crossed. But Fargo discovered that one of the horses was about to throw a shoe on his right foreleg. It was all he needed to know.

When he got back to camp the girl was up, wondering where he had gone. A few hours later they had ridden to within a short distance of Oroville, and it was here he left her.

"I'll be looking for you, Fargo."

"Good enough," he said, grinning gently at her.

"I have a strong feeling you'll find Uncle Jay."

She was pouting a little, but not out of irritation. For an instant he almost regretted his decision to go it alone, but it was gone almost before it touched him. She looked terrific sitting the little roan in her tight britches and fresh blouse, with the low neckline inviting his eyes to the superb mounds just tantalizing inches away from his hands.

He said nothing more. There was nothing more to say. He turned the Ovaro and pointed him north. He expected to reach Piney Creek during the night.

5

"Step right up, ladies and gents, and get your two-bit bottle of Dr. Elihu Forepaugh's Special Elixir! I repeat; this miraculous beverage is famed throughout the whole of the Great American West! It is held in awe by the entire medical profession not only in this country but all over Europe! Known all over the world as the People's Friend, it is unquestionably the greatest family medicine of the age!"

The intrepid "Doctor" Forepaugh held up one of the bottles as he spoke. A dozen more stood in a row on the table at his side. Behind him the circus wagon shone in all its brilliance under the morning sun. It was the Fourth of July, and the crowd numbered about three dozen; the entire "population" of Piney Creek trading post and environs, notably the Quarter Hitch cowboys, as well as the motley group of some dozen Indians who stood to one side and slightly to the rear of the crowd listening to and watching the strange antics of the extraordinary man with the beaver top hat, black broadcloth coat with satin lapels and brass buttons, and huge gold rings, one on each little finger. The red-skinned members of the small gathering were the residents and transients of Tipi Town, the Indian village on the other side of the slender creek that ribboned past the rear of the post building on its way south; no one particularly knew to where. These tribal folk were known to the whites as blanket Indians, or, by other Indians living out on the plains or in the mountains as Hang-Around-the-Forts.

Fargo was standing at the edge of the crowd, fascinated by Doc's performance. The little man was flamboyantly in command of his audience, and loving it all the way.

"Taken internally the elixir will cure the cholera, burns, swelled joints, boils, ringworm, indigestion. It will put an end to consumption, decline, asthma, colds, and night sweats. Used externally it is equally efficacious! Have you a lame horse? Has your child suffered physical injury? This fabulous nostrum may be applied to any part of the body. It is made from a secret formula of pure vegetable compounds. Try it! Try it—and join those numerous happy ones who have become our steady customers! Step right up, and don't be afraid to buy more than one bottle! Remember that prudence is the mother of satisfaction. Lay in a goodly supply!"

Doc's stentorian voice rang through the little group as the wattles beneath his chin shook with intensity; his iron forefinger, raised to heaven, insisted on the beneficence of the elixir, the value of clean living, and the path of righteousness. Fargo smiled at how easily Doc got carried away with his own rhetoric and the excitement of his pitch. He was without question a practiced thespian.

It had been a surprise when he discovered the medicine show and circus at Piney Creek; he'd thought they were heading for Oroville.

"I just thought we'd do it this way," Candy O'Hara explained to him when he asked. Only it was no explanation as far as Fargo was concerned.

He had arrived late the night before and had camped along the creek. One of the first people he'd run into in the morning was Candy. She'd been delighted to see him, though also surprised at the unexpected encounter.

"Couldn't stay away from me, huh Fargo?" Her eyes had sparkled with laughter as she looked up into his face. "Will you be here awhile with us?"

"Depends," he said. There was something in her brash attitude that caught him. He had the definite feeling that she was covering something. At the same time the invitation in her eyes and in the undulation of her body said more to him then a whole book of words.

Doc and the colonel had been equally delighted to see Fargo again, urging him to stay on for the show.

"Thought you were heading for Oro," Fargo had said, fishing for something more definite than Candy had given him.

"We were." Doc hooked his thumbs in his red vest and expanded his little chest. "We were heading for Oro, but by way of this mighty metropolis." He coughed out a bright laugh. "This Baghdad on the Great American Plains!" His hand swept in a semicircle to include the log building which housed the trading post proper, the half-dozen sagging shacks that lurked near it, and Tipi Town with its dozen or so tents. Doc shook his jowls as he intoned his words benignly and the colonel folded in rasping laughter.

"Aren't you going to set up the whole circus?" Fargo had asked, noticing that only the main "singing" wagon had been opened up with its platform, supporting the table and bottles of elixir.

"Not enough customers," Doc explained. "Generally—as a rule we just do the medicine show. In these small places God seems to have forgotten," he added with a roll of his eyes. "Card tricks. Fortunes. Such shenanigans as entice the populace." His hands embraced the crowd. "Not what you'd call numerous—or intelligent for that matter—but a crowd's a crowd. And we bring them something. We do not bring them nothing after all. And—uh . . ." He leaned toward the big man with the black hair and unruly forelock, his elbow nudging Fargo's arm, and dropped his voice to a confiding tone. "And the girls. The girls, Fargo! You see, Candy's end of the show is—uh— also, shall we say, attractive!" His little eyes lit up; he suddenly cracked his knuckles. Fargo again caught the rank odor of elixir on his breath. "Eh, Fargo? Might try a little—later on."

The colonel was beaming in his white buckskin suit with the long fringes. He had evidently gotten over his initial competitiveness and resentment of Fargo and was now at his most cordial.

"You've been here before then," Fargo had observed mildly.

"Oh yes, we travel the circuit," said the colonel. "Virginia City is our best location. Sometimes we hit Reno and Carson City. Mostly it's the mining camps and an occasional town with the hair on;

97

like this place sometimes of an evening." He was nodding toward a group of young men with trail-worn Stetson hats, dusty clothing, and tied-down handguns who had just ridden in. "The boys, I am told, like their funnin'."

Doc was chuckling. "They say the Quarter Hitch nailed this town together with bullets one Saturday night."

"Good I missed it," said the colonel lugubriously. "I'd've had to discipline it some." He turned confidingly to Fargo. "Used to be town marshal at Honeyville, Kansas. While back. Awhile back," he repeated, and reached for his chewing tobacco, first brushing his hair out of his eyes. It seemed to Fargo that the curls had grown longer and wilder.

"The colonel might put on his wild-West show later. If the boys are still sober," Doc said, squinting into the sun. "But the main thing we're having is the boxing."

"You mean Irish Packy?" Fargo remembered the big man with the shoulders like a bison and hands like shovels.

"Irish Packy will do his act. Taking on any and all comers at his usual price."

"Sometime he'll carry a feller," Clyde Toole put in. "Give the crowd a run for their money."

"And you boys—and ladies," he added as Candy O'Hara joined them, "take side bets."

"How else is a honest girl gonna make a decent living in this cruel world?" wailed Candy with a sly smirk. "Don't answer it!" she flashed out as the doc started to tell her. And the group broke into chortling laughter.

Following Doc's opening medical spiel, the rest

of the morning was taken up with acrobatics, some bronc riding with the riders of the Quarter Hitch competing with the old former bronc stomper Elbows McFowles, horse racing, card tricks by the colonel, and the luscious Aphrodite, who also told fortunes, and viewing of the caged animals. When Fargo asked about the "talking" bear and "singing" snakes, Candy and Doc told him they had the croup and so that part of the show had been canceled.

"*All* the snakes?" he asked, suppressing a grin.

"All that knows how," said Candy, frowning hard at Toole, who, Fargo remembered, was the alleged "ventriloquist" for the act.

"It's more of a show than we planned," Candy told him, "and the boys have done their best in your honor, and in thanks for helping us with the Indians, and all."

"I appreciate it," the big man said.

"And on account of it is the glorious Fourth," Doc said.

It was at a moment following the horse racing that Fargo saw Irish Packy O'Corrigan approaching. The man looked bigger and nastier than ever.

"Comin' to the prizefightin', Fargo?"

"Might take a look-see."

"That about all?" The big man's face had turned mahogany red, and his eyes gleamed with hatred.

"Maybe." Fargo was looking at Irish closely, sizing up the muscles, the way he moved, the manner in which he stood, and how he spaced his feet. He could hear the deep surliness and he knew that O'Corrigan was seething with jealousy from the night he had spotted him with Candy.

In fact, it was the very next thing that the sneering man came out with.

"I'll be looking for you to show some guts and try to last a round. Might even carry you a round or two so they get their money's worth."

" 'Preciate it." Fargo shifted his weight forward a little.

"Might like to try proving yourself to the womenfolk by lasting a few minutes."

"Might." Fargo realized the man was built like a railroad car. He must have a weakness, he reasoned. Everybody did. There wasn't a man alive who didn't favor some place in his body; his weak place. But the big Irish seemed truly impregnable.

"I'll look for you then," O'Corrigan said.

"I'll be seeing you." Fargo was watching the little pulse in the fighter's throat, but he knew it wasn't that. What then?

"Won't be no women you'll be screwing for a while, Fargo, when I get through with you."

Fargo grinned without changing the ice-blue stare of his eyes. So it was going to be that kind of a fight. Good enough. "And when I get through with you, Packy my boy, you not only won't be able to screw, you won't even be able to play with it."

"Go fuck yourself, Fargo!"

"Best offer so far today."

"You want to settle it now?"

"Anytime. Anyplace."

"Better in front of people so's they see what a fucker you are." And he turned on his heel and walked off.

It was in that instant when Packy O'Corrigan

turned that Fargo saw what he'd been looking for.

The ring was pitched on turf not far from the little collection of buildings and consisted of four posts driven into the ground, around which two strands of lariat rope, about three feet apart were wound. Doc Forepaugh did the announcing, introducing Irish Packy O'Corrigan as the "Heavyweight Champion of Ireland and Californy! Packy will take on any and all comers, offering two dollars a round if you stay one round, and that amount doubling for subsequent rounds!"

"And what about if himself gets knocked on his big fat ass?" queried the old stomper who had raced against the Quarter Hitch boys—and lost. Fargo could see that Elbows McFowles was almost sloshing with booze imbibed at the log trading post. "Shit, I got me a notion to fisticuff the big bastard meself!" He was an old man, resembling an aged swamper Fargo had once run across in a Denver saloon: yet somehow with some other quality besides age and defeat in him. Yes, the old boy still had spirit: he still had guts. It wasn't only the liquor talking.

The gathering loved it. While the enormous Corrigan peeled down to his trunks, they stood in the broiling sun, cheering Elbows, who was waving his bony fists at "The Champion" from outside the ring.

"Any takers!" cried Doc. "Do I see one of you young men wanting to feel his oats!" And he pointed toward a group of Quarter Hitch riders who, like the old man, had indulged themselves in strong refreshment. But not so much that they were foolhardy. The crowd finally subsided when Doc announced that nobody "under the influence of alcohol" would be accepted as an opponent for Packy O'Corrigan, "or he might get killed!"

"Go sober up, Elbows!" someone shouted.

The little old man stood there just outside the ring, working his jaws like a squirrel worrying a nut. "By jingo, they allus find some excuse, by God!"

And the crowd roared.

There was a sudden commotion at the edge of the small crowd and heads turned to see the big man with the lake-blue eyes pushing his way toward the ring.

"Ah!" cried Doc. "Here comes a worthy challenger! Skye Fargo, heavyweight champion of—of, where you from, Fargo?" As the crowd roared with laughter.

"Why not Piney Creek?"

"The heavyweight champion of Piney Creek!"

Irish Packy spat into the dirt and strutted slowly around the inside of the ropes flexing his huge muscles.

But when Fargo climbed into the ring and stripped to the waist a gasp went up. There wasn't an ounce of extra flesh or fat on his lean, lionlike body.

Looking over the crowd now he saw Candy O'Hara staring at him from the side of the singing wagon. Damn woman ought to be happy, he reflected ruefully, getting up a fight on her own account.

Meanwhile, to the incredulity of all, Elbows McFowles had climbed into the ring.

"I'll referee this here," he announced, and began shadow boxing around the enclosure, finally tripping himself and falling in a heap while the crowd was nearly brought to its knees at the high jinks. Doc was right in the spirit of it, counting over the fallen gladiator, his arm sweeping up and down like a scythe.

Elbows didn't stir. He was curled up like a little ball, snoring blissfully and loudly in the center of the ring. At Doc's order two men came and removed him, while he slept on, to the incredible hilarity of the audience, who, realizing that Fargo was no hick trying to earn a dollar and prove his courage, were eagerly placing bets on the outcome.

At last, with the ring clear, Doc, officiating also as referee, called the fighters to him. He was dressed for the occasion, having dispensed with his broadcloth coat and red vest. In shirt-sleeves with gold garters on the arms, he leaned toward the two fighters. Fargo noticed with amusement the red bandanna handkerchief sticking out of his pocket, stiff as a rabbit's ear.

"There will be no butting, biting, hair pulling, kicking, or gouging," Doc declared. "A round ends when the man is down, and he better make it to scratch or he is out. Them is London Prize Ring Rules. Let me see your shoes; no spikes. And let me see those hands."

He examined the hands for any hidden "equalizers" such as rock or metal. "Any fouling I give the fight to the other man. Remember, what I says goes. Fargo, Packy—you'll fight square; and the money, the money is as announced." He paused, clearing his nose and throat of phlegm and spitting hugely, almost drowning a small mouse who for some inexplicable reason had appeared at ringside. "You men got any last words?"

"I bet a hundred dollars on whipping his hairy ass," Irish Packy said.

"I'll raise you a hundred," said Fargo.

The ringsiders heard it and bedlam broke loose as the betting intensified. It took several minutes to get it all straightened out, with Doc shouting for order. It was the colonel who managed to bring order out of the frenzied financial transactions, and when the bets were finally down he nodded to Doc. Everyone by now was soaking with perspiration.

The sun was a blister in the sky as the fighters went to their corners at Doc's order. The eager spectators pressed against the two strands of rope and ring stakes and Doc had to keep shouting at them to move back. The betting favored Irish, who was bigger and was a professional fighter.

But by now Elbows McFowles had concluded his brief nap and suddenly appeared, weaving into Fargo's corner.

"You need professional help here, boy," he announced, breathing whiskey violently on everyone within range, including Fargo. "Stay away from him. Wear the sonofabitch down; don't let him get close to you."

"I'll handle it, Elbows," Fargo said amiably. "Have a seat."

"You want a drink, Fargo?"

"Later."

"He'll fight you dirty. I know the bastard." And for a moment the little old man straightened up, almost sober.

But Fargo had no time for dwelling on such

interesting observations. He was planning his strategy, knowing that speed was his chief advantage, and so he had better not let the giant get his arms around him.

Now, at a signal from Doc, the colonel picked up a singletree and banged the bottom of a bucket rapidly several times. And the fight was on!

Fargo moved easily out of his corner while O'Corrigan charged across the ring. The huge man began throwing punches, trying at the same time to work in close to his opponent. Fargo received a tremendous right to the chest and another to his left ear. Both blows were numbing. The next thing, Irish Packy had closed and had his arms around him in a bear hug. In a trice he had backheeled Fargo to the ground, landing right on top of him, kneeing in the crotch to boot. Thus ended round one. The crowd feverishly began shrieking new bets.

Resting for a moment Fargo realized that the referee's admonition against fouling did not include Packy's almost breaking his balls.

Elbows, his arms flailing, rasped out advice with the speed of a repeating rifle. "Stay away from the bugger! Keep him off balance! Feint him so he comes in to you, then let him have it right in the balls! Use yer knee, yer elbows!"

"Time!" shrieked the colonel, banging the singletree on the bucket. The sound was barely heard above the din of the small crowd.

Fargo came sharp to scratch, driving a vicious right into Packy O'Corrigan's kidney, another to his solar plexus. He forged in, and instantly found himself wrapped in another bear hug, but this time he ran his beard stubble like a coarse file

105

over his opponent's eyes until O'Corrigan's grip loosened and Fargo broke away.

They circled each other, Doc having difficulty keeping out of the way. Meantime, Elbows was screaming advice to Fargo and profanities at O'Corrigan.

"O'Corrigan, yer fly's open, you asshole!"

"Packy, you pigshit Irish, you, you got to sit down to piss!"

Suddenly Irish Packy drove in, slashing his fingernails just above Fargo's eyes. But the Trailsman was getting his opponent's measure.

He stuck his left, stiff as a pole, into the big man's swollen face, ducked a smashing right, weaved in close, and struck like lightning—in the belly, the rib cage, the throat; and then setting the other man up straight with his left, he smashed him twice in the left shoulder, paralyzing O'Corrigan's arm and causing him to turn away. Fargo heard the little click of the Irishman's trick knee—the weakness he had noted that morning. It was the moment he had been waiting for, and he now drove in with his opponent weaker and off balance for just that second. It was enough. A terrific right to the ear, followed by a vicious blow to the kidney, and another in the ribs.

The Heavyweight Champion of Ireland and California bent almost double in pain and exhaustion, and now Fargo coolly drilled him just behind the ear. Irish Packy O'Corrigan fell like a poleaxed steer. And for a hideous moment Fargo thought the rabbit punch had killed him.

The crowd felt it, too, and was suddenly silent. No one was going to make it to scratch after a wallop like that.

Fargo, sucking in the heated air, walked quietly to his corner, when all at once the little man who had made himself his second rushed to embrace him, all but leaping into his arms and nearly knocking Fargo off his feet.

"You done it! You whipped his big ass, by God! I knowed it! Knowed when I first seed you! Knowed you was a fighter! Shit, boy, we'll go to the coast, go back East; we'll wipe the country with them fists of yourn! I'll manage you, teach you the tricks. We'll be in clover! I know the tricks! I'll learn you the whole shit and shebang of the whole entire art of fisticuffs!"

Elbows fell suddenly to coughing, doubled over, hawking, sneezing and wheezing, gasping for air, and again Fargo had the terrible thought that someone was about to die on the spot. But Elbows recovered, as did Irish Packy O'Corrigan, aided in both cases by generous quantities of Dr. Forepaugh's Elixir rushed to the occasion by the grateful public.

Finally, as he ducked out of the ring, Fargo said, "It was a good fight, Elbows."

"That it was, lad. That it was." Elbows McFowles' grin ran all over his gristly old face. "And ye know what, my boy . . . ?"

"What?"

"I'll be proud to let the new champeen of Ireland and Californy buy me a drink!"

Fargo, his face hurting more than a little, burst out laughing. And as he moved through the crowd of well-wishers he saw a woman standing over near the doorway of one of the shacks. For a moment he was struck by her resemblance to Constance Bogardus. But it was a fleeting thought only, for he was swept away by the exultant crowd, who all but carried him to the bar.

Fargo was painfully aware of the battering from Packy O'Corrigan's big fists, but he felt good. The action had stirred something in him and he was invigorated. He finally managed to push away from the throng of well-wishers and winning bettors and walked down to the livery barn to check the Ovaro.

The big pinto nickered when he saw Fargo, pawed the floor of his stall. Fargo led him outside and began giving him a rubdown and currying. He wanted to think, and felt too the need for some simple activity. He was thinking of the woman he had seen watching the fight from the doorway of the trading post, the one who looked like Connie Bogardus.

He worked slowly with the Ovaro, taking extra time because he wanted to make sure that the livery would be empty. Finally when the hostler left for supper, he led the pinto back inside.

There were a half-dozen horses in the big barn with the low roof. He worked quickly, checking the hooves of each for any sign that would compare with those he had seen the day before on the trail. There was nothing.

He had walked outside when he had an idea and walked over to the big watering trough. Here the ground was much softer, and there were many hoof prints of horses. He looked closely for several minutes before he finally saw it. It was quite clear, the print he had seen where the four riders had lost his and Melissa's trail, the horse with the loose shoe.

Fargo spent another several minutes covering the whole area outside the livery, but there was nothing further until he saw another print followed by three more outside a lean-to on the far side of the livery which was clearly the blacksmith's shop. So, the horse had been shod. But from that place on, the tracks were too dim, for the ground was bare of grass and the wind had already whipped dust to cover any sign. All the same, his hunch had been right. Whoever had been following their trail had come to Piney Creek, and was either here now or on the way to someplace else. More than likely he was a Quarter Hitch rider.

It was still only afternoon, though getting on toward sundown when he led the Ovaro to where he had camped the night before. He picketed the big black and white horse and lay down on his bedroll. Then, on an impulse he got up, shucked off his clothes, and walked into the creek.

The icy water braced him, and with his skin tingling he came out of the water and ran to his bedding and lay down naked. He had decided he would take a short nap since it was not yet nightfall and then later visit the trading-post bar to see what he could pick up in the way of leads to solving the problem of Uncle Jason and his family.

He was just dozing, letting his mind walk through the different questions, the scenes he had encountered with Rivers, Bogardus, and Melissa and Connie, trying to piece it together, when he smelled her. He smelled her even before he heard the sound of her footsteps. For a split second he wished it was Connie Bogardus, even though he knew it wasn't. Opening his eyes, he looked up at the evening sky, spreading down to the land like a velvet blanket.

"Thought I'd come and congratulate the winner," Candy O'Hara said. And as her eyes drew toward his enormous erection she added, "The both of you."

"Fighting makes a man horny," Fargo said, looking up at her as she stepped closer.

She knelt down and his eyes moved right into the opening of her shirt, down the valley of her big, taut mounds while her own eyes were on his hard member. "Fargo, don't kid me. You're horny all day and all night long."

"Not all the time," he said.

"Hah! When not? When aren't you?"

She had slipped down beside him and he reached over and began unbuttoning her shirt.

"I'll show you how to find out when I'm not horny," he said as she helped him remove her shirt.

Leaning down, she slipped her eager lips over his hard thing and murmured with joy.

"That's one way to make you shut up," he said. "And it's also the way to find out when I'm not horny," he said as she began sucking him in long, slow, strokes.

The trading post proper was a ramshackle log building with additions tacked on at random as the need had arisen. It covered most of a large rectangle of ground that had once been covered with grass. But with the traffic of horses and wagons and people the area around the log structure had become a dust trap whenever the wind blew, which was not infrequently. The grass that grew nearby was stubbled and yellow; it wasn't until one reached the creek that there was any green.

Inside the building's main room a bar made of planking set on crates ran almost the length of one side. The floor was uneven planking, the ceiling low. There were counters across from the bar, some of them glass-covered; they contained a variety of articles for the trapper, the prospector, the cowhand, the general traveler. There was jawbreaker candy, tobacco, straight razors, knives, guns and ammo, and other assorted equipment for the trail and outdoor struggle for existence. In the center of the room was a big potbellied stove. Interestingly, or so Fargo thought, the stove was more or less shaped like the proprietor of the trading post. Floyd Dustin was a large man with all his weight in his hips, feet that pointed way out so that he waddled like a huge duck, and with a long thin neck and head that resembled a stovepipe. He had a large wart just above the bridge of his nose, and it was difficult for certain people not to look at it while talking to him. Fargo didn't have that problem, however, when he ordered a drink that evening for himself and for Elbows McFowles who greeted him just inside the door.

"Figgered you'd show," the little old man said genially, escorting Fargo to the bar.

"Figured you'd find me again," Fargo shot back pleasantly. "Kind of gloomy, isn't it?" He squinted up at the coal oil lamp suspended from the ceiling.

"Be thankful," someone said at his elbow, and the remark was accompanied by a throaty chuckle.

Following some nods and remarks of recognition and congratulation, Fargo and his companion sat at a table at one end of the room. Fargo looked about, his eyes growing accustomed to the dingy atmosphere. Some of the Quarter Hitch boys were in evidence, not too clearly defined in the pale, lemon-colored light.

"They'll liquor theirselves," Elbows McFowles observed. "Then like as not ventilate some of the town with their pop pistols."

"Appears there's no law to argue it," Fargo said.

The old man lowered one lid, sniffed. "Oh, there is the law, a bona-fide marshal. He come here I'd say couple of months back, and shortly he took on the job *permanent*." He turned his head to look right at Fargo with no expression at all on his face. "You'll find him planted out back of the livery."

Fargo grinned at the old man's wry humor. "What kind of outfit is the Quarter Hitch?" he asked. "What do they handle there? Beef?"

"About three hundred head of beef cattle, and horses. And they put up hay and sells it I have been told. Shit, you get fifty cents a pound on hay, and that is money."

"Good way to turn a profit," Fargo agreed.

"See, the outfit is protected by the valley and holds grass all winter long, so you can't do better than that when you need feed. Hell, Bogardus sells to Virginia City, Reno, and Gold Hill, and anyone else he can."

"Bogardus!" Fargo felt as though he'd been shaken out of his sleep.

"Grady Bogardus. It's his outfit."

"I thought Bogardus was in land and mining."

"Reckon he is; him and Connie, his wife. She is the relative of some kind or other of Conrad Rivers. You've heard of him."

Fargo nodded. "But why a ranch? Seems to me that's small potatoes next to those mines."

"Likes horses. Got some of the best horseflesh in the country. Always trading and buying and selling."

"Races them?"

"I reckon." The old man's brow wrinkled. "Though now you mention it, I don't believe I ever noticed any racing Bogardus done with his animals. But then . . ." He shrugged, reached for his glass of whiskey.

Fargo looked down at the brown fluid in his glass and lifted it to the light as though examining it. Actually, he was studying a man who had just walked in and who looked familiar. Yet he couldn't place him. Thin, with a long bony nose and big-knuckled hands. Virginia City? Laramie? He couldn't remember. He lowered the glass, turned to Elbows McFowles. "Is that why his men pack all that hardware? Those horses worth a lot of money?"

"It's the robberies and killings. You've for sure heard tell. Owl-hooters are thicker than bedbugs. Man can't take his poke a dozen yards from his claim 'fore he gets stiffed by some goddam gunswift or some bastard with a skinning knife. Shit, Fargo, around this country they got more hold-ups and murders than you get in a fucking war. Bogardus, he's got the right idea." He paused. " 'Course now with the railroad coming directly it'll finish the stage business. They'll ship all the ore by rail in armored cars."

"End the holdups for sure," Fargo agreed. "At least, the big stuff." The big man looked at his little companion thoughtfully. "I don't see you packing anything."

"Me?" The face meshed into a thousand wrinkles and the eyes gleamed. "I ain't got nothin' for the buggers to swipe. And I got to admit, I ain't fast like I used to be. Shit, I used to be greased lightning; could light a lucifer stuck across the room there with one bullet." He coughed out a little ball of laughter.

"Lost my ability howsomever when I took my vacation in Folsom some years back."

"Prison's a good place for a vacation I have heard," Fargo said amiably. "Though I'd rather the mountains."

"Spent two years in Folsom for lying to the judge."

"Lying? Two years?"

The little man sniffed. "I said I was innocent and the judge he found out I was guilty."

Fargo chuckled at the way Elbows told his story. By now it was late and the room was almost deserted. The high jinks that Elbows had predicted hadn't taken place. Fargo was not sorry for that. He was thinking of Connie Bogardus, thinking that the woman he had seen at the fight could likely have been her.

And then suddenly it struck him with the force of a blow that the lean man at the bar with the long, bony nose was the stage driver he and Constance Bogardus had seen whipping the stage out from the Wells, Fargo office in Virginia City, not long ago. Well, he reasoned, not much so wrong with that—at least on the surface.

Now he let his attention fall on Floyd Dustin, the post sutler, who was across the room at the counter loading a big gunnysack with ammunition, tobacco, and some other articles.

"Call it a night, Elbows," he said standing up.

"Good enough. Next time it'll be on me," Elbows mumbled as they went outside.

Fargo grinned at the way the little man had put it on him.

When he walked outside the moon was up and he stood for a moment studying the sky. A door opened off to his right and light streamed out onto the ground. He half turned to see Floyd Dustin appear with the heavily loaded gunnysack. Now, silent as a shadow, a small figure came into the light from another direction. Fargo saw the headband, the long black hair hanging down in two braids over the girl's or woman's shoulders. She moved with dazzling grace, young and strong. Dustin had put the sack down and turned back into the building, but the woman had crossed the light just before he shut the door, and Fargo had a good view of her.

"Them Injuns," Elbows said at his side. "They ain't allowed in the inside. So Dustin he serves 'em out the back. It ain't against the law. Just he can't sell them the whiskey. But the whites, they don't like 'em on the inside, and Dustin, he don't want trouble."

"Quarter Hitch straight north about?" Fargo asked as he watched the Indian woman disappear in the night.

"I could show you," the little man said eagerly. "I ain't much for words and maps like."

Fargo studied it a moment. There was something in his companion's voice even more than the eagerness that caught him. "I could maybe save you some time," Elbows McFowles said.

"I'm in no hurry."

"But I can see you are not here to enjoy the scenery neither," the other said astutely.

Fargo grinned.

"I got let go by Candy O'Hara. They don't want me no more."

"How come?"

"Maybe 'cause I lost the horse race. Maybe on account I seen her bedded with Grady Bogardus—not meaning to," he added quickly.

"I'll see you at sunup," Fargo said, and disappeared into the night.

After checking the Ovaro, he stretched out on his bedroll. He didn't feel like undressing. He didn't feel he could let that much go. Somehow, in some way, he knew this was not the moment to let his guard down.

6

Twice during the night he got up and moved from where he had been resting. At one point he heard a horse nicker over at the medicine-show encampment, and the mild jangle of harness. And when he rose to investigate, he found his suspicions verified as he watched the wagons pulling away from Piney Creek.

At dawn Elbows McFowles was right there, riding a little strawberry roan with a cast in the left eye.

"Wagons is gone," he said lugubriously. "They must've took off early."

"That I know," the Trailsman said.

"We still heading for the Quarter Hitch?"

"After I take a look at those wagon tracks," Fargo said, tightening the cinch on the Ovaro and then stepping into the saddle.

In a moment they were at the medicine-show campsite and Fargo had stepped down from the pinto and was examining the ground and surrounding vegetation.

"You read the sign like a damn Injun," Elbows

said, leaning forward on the pommel of his scarred saddle.

The Trailsman was squatting over some wagon ruts, and now, still squatting, he turned his head toward the little man on the roan horse and said, "Interesting."

"You see something?" Elbows' small head perked up like a rooster on the prowl.

"See a lot. One thing; tell me why those wagons are so loaded leaving here, I mean a whole lot more than when they came in."

Elbows pursed his lips, squinted, scratched under his ear. "Maybe they bought out Dustin's stock." But it was said as humor, not serious fact.

"Something heavy," Fargo said, speaking to the tracks he was studying. "These here, they're deeper than those over yonder. These men were carrying something heavy, and they loaded whatever it was in the wagon there."

He stood up, a stem of grass in his mouth, and he remained where he was, swing-hipped, contemplating the campsite, trying to put the pieces together. Why Piney Creek? Why Oroville, which according to Melissa Rivers was even less of a community?

"You going after?" Elbows suddenly broke the long silence.

Fargo raised his head, his face clearing. "Know something, Elbows?"

"Know a lot, I do, but you tell it."

"Thing is, as I see it, never do what's expected of you."

"So we ain't going after."

Fargo grinned. "We are going to have a look at the Quarter Hitch." He stepped easily into the saddle. And cocked his eye at his companion. "That is, if you've still a mind to."

They headed north and west, the big man's lake-blue eyes searching the country around him. He had easily picked up the trail he'd been seeking and was gratified to find that at least for the present the tracks of the Indian he had seen behind the trading post went in the same direction as the trail to the Quarter Hitch.

Toward the end of the forenoon the Indian pony tracks took another trail, veering to the left, toward the mountains.

Fargo dismounted and, squatting, studied some prints where the Indian pony had stood while the woman had gotten down. One print was especially clear, telling him by the shape that she was Shoshone. The Trailsman had made an exhaustive study of footprints. He knew the tribes by their moccasins, even as he knew them by their manner of cutting their hair.

"What you see?" Elbows asked. "I seen you following sign, but I don't believe an eagle could read what you been readin'."

"That Indian I saw outside Dustin's; she went down this trail here. She's Shoshone. Couldn't quite tell the whole of it in the light last night."

"The Quarter Hitch is other side of that big butte."

"We'll make it come nightfall then."

They rode in silence again, and midway through the afternoon Fargo drew rein at a stream bank. It was cooler now, he realized, feeling the change on the skin of his hands and face. He sat there without dismounting, pausing to listen to the exquisite song of a meadowlark. As they rested their horses, Fargo with his Sharps lying across the saddletree, they suddenly saw a huge brownish-yellow monster on the other side of the creek. The big grizzly was ambling across the trail ahead, moving with bulky grace, its great coat like waves of prairie grass in a magnificent flow of light and color. The animal was oblivious to the two humans watching him; they were well away from his dim eyesight and upwind from his keen sense of smell.

"Could take Mr. Grizzly easy with the Sharps," Elbows muttered pensively.

"What for?"

"Just thinkin' of the time I seen a grizzly and a badger have at it. Boy, that was some fight. Badger took off half Mr. Grizzly's nose 'fore he got hisself squashed to nothing. I mean he chewed that bear's nose right off in half!"

Fargo sat the pinto, watching with admiration and wonder the great beast on its way to something not yet known. He leaned back now in the stock saddle, with his hand on the skirt behind the cantle. Across the creek and down beyond the valley the snowcapped peaks looked eternal as judgment of all that lay before them. He waited, listening until the grizzly was no longer audible.

Now he scanned the horizon, sniffed the air for any strange odor, such as Indian or wild animal, or especially, white men. He loved the vast grandeur of his world: the mountains crowned with snow, the valleys laden with berries, the meadows lush with thick green grass and silence, the prairies with their antelope and buffalo. For him the beauty was heartbreaking; the raw beauty of this world of wild things: the weasel, wolf, mink, cougar, wolverine, grizzly, bobcat, hawk and eagle; ferocious and ready to kill; and the rabbit and deer and elk and buffalo and antelope, and the birds in their feathered beauty.

Meanwhile, Elbows had been filling him in on the Quarter Hitch. Grady Bogardus had the place a few years now, raised and sold horses, bought and traded a few. Raised cattle too. Sold hay, and had hired a crew of some pretty tough boys. Most of this Fargo already knew, but the little man fleshed it out.

"Like I said, they'll steal anything around the Comstock, not stopping at prize horseflesh," Elbows told him. "Bogardus got his interests to handle; why all the armaments?"

It was reaching the end of the day when Fargo suddenly pulled on the reins and stepped quickly out of his saddle.

"What's up?" Elbows had been following close behind and swerved the roan out of the trail so he wouldn't bump into the Ovaro.

"Track I been looking for." Fargo was studying something on the ground.

"Don't see nothing."

"It's there. That horse that threw its shoe, then got a new one with the little chip on the outside. I couldn't quite make it out before, but this print is clear as my own hand."

"Meaning?"

"Meaning one of the boys following me recently, though not having much luck, is riding toward the Quarter Hitch with this bunch. They'll be there by now for sure." He paused, his keen eyes scanning the country as he stood very still, not making a sound himself that would interfere with his listening.

"I do believe we're pretty close," Fargo said, presently.

"Butte's yonder and the outfit's just beyond."

"You smell it?"

"Don't smell nothin', except this here horse. Only wish I had a woman to smell. That'd be something all right, by God."

"You can smell the cookfire," Fargo said.

"Maybe they'll invite us to eat."

"Sure." He mounted the pinto and they rode more quickly now. "There'll more than likely be point men out," Fargo said. "If Bogardus is that careful." And he was wondering just why Grady Bogardus was so careful. He turned toward Elbows who had moved up beside him. "I've heard Bogardus was in land speculation, and I've heard he was in mining with Conrad Rivers."

"He is into everything," Elbows said with a wet sniff. "Including Candy O'Hara's drawers like I told you, and anybody else he can get at. Don't know how that pretty little wife of his stands for it."

"Know her?" Fargo asked, his thoughts sweeping to the beautiful Constance.

"Wish I did."

They had reached the near side of the big butte and had now started to ride around it.

"See that stand of box elders over there?" Fargo said.

"How could I miss it?" snorted Elbows. "Just 'cause I am now and again a mite loose on my pins—like when under the influence—don't mean

I am plumb dumb, Mr. Skye Fargo." And Fargo had to grin at the snappy little man.

"I want you to hole up there."

"And yourself, you'll be ridin' in on your lonesome, I expect."

"Tonight I'll go afoot. Tomorrow—we'll see."

They had reached the stand of box elders and now entered into the thick growth. It would be a good place for Elbows to be staked out in case he needed him. The trees were close together, and there was a lot of brush.

"What good am I to be doing out here?" Elbows asked, his tone sour.

"I need you on my back trail. I am leaving you this Remington, and here's a Deane and Adams. You can handle them?"

"I kin handle any firearm, no matter the size, with equal dexterity in either hand," the little man said, drawing himself up in his saddle with awesome dignity. "Didn't tell you why I happened to get into Folsom, did I? Well, it was for shootin' a outlaw, feller name of Barney Mahoney. The scourge of California, he was known as in the newspapers. I drilled the sonofabitch right up his right nostril. The .45 slug entered his brain and carried that brain right on out the top of his head, disintegrating same in a swamp of blood and innards! By God, Fargo, he had the drop on me, and I outdrawed him and shot him deader 'n hell!"

Fargo grinned. "And the judge only gave you two years for that?"

"Well, I got the two years for manslaughter, but the judge didn't lay it on on account of I argued it to being self-defense since he had the drop on me, and it was simply a altercation over cards; and anyways, the sonofabitch died of a heart attack, I told the judge, and he half believed me—'fore he got hit by my bullet, that is. He died of fright, was how it was; when he saw how fast I outdrew him! But . . ." He shrugged. "I still got two years."

"You should have been a lawyer," Fargo said.

"Used to be," the little man said, his face straight as a fistful of aces.

It didn't take long for Elbows to settle into the place Fargo picked, a spot that gave him the best visibility on anyone approaching.

"You stay awake now," Fargo said as he turned to leave the stand of trees.

"Nothing to worry about," Elbows said.

"You got any whiskey on you?"

The little man's hand raced to his pocket. "Why, sure. You want a snort?"

"Hand it over."

Elbows McFowles' jaw dropped. "Hand it over!"

"That's what I said. I don't want you getting blistered out here and doing me no good and maybe even harm when I need you."

"Fargo, I swear I . . ."

Fargo stood like a tree in front of the knobby little man, holding out his hand, for the bottle. Reluctantly, like a small child, Elbows handed him the bottle of whiskey.

As Fargo slipped it into his saddlebag Elbows said, "You'll leave me a mite, Fargo, my friend?"

"It isn't good for you to drink so much," Fargo said. "You think I didn't notice you takin' it while we were riding? I could smell you if I was a mile away."

With a nod, he left the forlorn former bronc stomper, gunman and outlaw, lawyer, circus handyman, saloon swamper, and half a dozen other things he'd claimed to have been, and led the Ovaro out of the little copse of trees.

The sun was halfway below the horizon when he rode around the butte and up a short rise. Before him lay the Quarter Hitch ranch houses and barn. He dismounted and, leaving the Ovaro picketed, walked partway along a line of cottonwoods which afforded him protection while he studied the layout below.

There were horse corrals and a number of good-looking young stuff cropping the feed in a fenced-in paddock. When the sun had gone down and the dark gave him cover, he slipped down to the ranch house and barn. It was still light enough for him to see, yet dark enough to cover his movements since he was careful.

He made it to the barn without mishap, although at one moment somebody came out of the bunkhouse to urinate and study the weather and then went back in. There didn't appear to be any guards posted, and he thought this curious in the light of Bogardus's supposed concern over robberies. In fact, Fargo was beginning to wonder what the real reason was for the heavily armed riders. The answer given by Elbows McFowles didn't ring right. It sounded like something given out by Bogardus simply to satisfy the curious.

It was pitch dark inside the barn and there was a strangely familiar smell. He stood quietly for a long time listening to a couple of horses feeding and stomping in their stalls, the scurrying of pack rats here and there, and the general sounds an old barn always makes. When he was sure it was safe he struck a lucifer and quickly took in his surroundings, trying to locate the source of the smell. He struck another match and then in the corner he saw the cans of paint. Crossing swiftly, he lit another match and studied the cans and brushes. The brushes were still wet.

Fargo stopped absolutely still again, listening. He knew that the only way to listen was to be quiet inside himself. And this he did. Then he crossed to the two horses in the stalls and gentling them, for they had begun to snort at his approach, he ran his hands slowly over their foreheads and down their legs. When his hands encountered the stickiness on one's leg and the other's forehead, he had found what he was looking for.

He lighted a half-dozen more matches, checked out the barn more completely, and then, placing all the burnt ends in his shirt pocket, slipped outside. Twenty minutes later he was in the stand of box elders with Elbows McFowles. The little man was wide-awake, which surprised him. But he was also pleased.

"Still got that bottle, Fargo, have you?"

"Yup. And I'm going to keep it."

"Couldn't we just have a little one?"

"Think of all you can have when we get back to Piney or someplace in one piece, and how otherwise, if we don't get back you'll not have any. You know in the place you're going to, Elbows, they don't have liquor."

"That is why I have lived this long, Fargo.

Knowing that has kept me this side of the grave for all my years."

Fargo took some dry jerked beef and a can of peaches from his bedroll. He was famished. Elbows had already eaten and now sat watching him.

"And tomorrow?" the little man asked.

"Tomorrow will take care of itself," Fargo said. "You sleep now. Then in a couple of hours you'll spell me on guard."

The day broke gently over the high country, the light penetrating the sky without a sound. Now the sunlight, growing stronger as it moved further into the great sky, also fell over the land, touching everything, yet caught by nothing.

It was early in the forenoon when the big man with the black hair and black Stetson hat rode the black-and-white pinto down the long draw into the valley that contained the Quarter Hitch ranch.

Fargo knew he was being watched, and when he rode up past the paddock with the dozen horses cropping at the good meadow grass, past the round horse corral where three young bays were frisking, and on up to the bunkhouse, he saw the riders coming in from the north at almost the same time that the bunkhouse door opened and three men wearing heavy hardware stepped out. Quickly Fargo cut his eye to the barn where two more men had appeared.

As he swung toward the direction of the main house, which like the bunkhouse was built of logs, the three stepped forward.

"Hold it, mister." The middle one was short, stocky, and his hand was close to the tied-down six-gun at his hip. His two companions flanked him. Fargo drew rein.

"What's your business? This here is private property."

"My business," the Trailsman said evenly, "is what I keep to myself until I am ready to speak it."

The stocky man's hand moved closer to his holstered weapon.

"I asked you a question, stranger!"

"And I gave you an answer. Now get out of my way." And Fargo suddenly kicked the Ovaro forward.

The three men were caught in surprise as the big horse bore down on them, and they had no chance to draw their weapons—especially since the rider had a big Colt .45 gripped in his right hand and an expression on his hard copper-colored face that wasn't about to argue the point.

Fargo realized the chance he had taken, but he knew that surprise and shock were necessary at such a moment. As he trotted the pinto up to the main house the door opened and a man stepped out. It was Grady Bogardus.

"Why it's Fargo, isn't it? Conrad Rivers told me about you. Come on in!" And turning to the surprised threesome, he called out. "Somebody take his horse." Turning back to Fargo, he said again, "Come on in. A surprise to see you, but a pleasant one." The tone was affable, even hearty.

Then Fargo played his ace. He had stepped down from the Ovaro, and with his eyes full on Grady Bogardus and in clear earshot of the three men who had walked up to where they were standing, he said, "Thought I'd come by, Bogardus, take your wife up on her invitation."

Grady Bogardus had a ruddy complexion; he was a handsome man in his thirties, strong-featured with hard, piercing green eyes; but at Fargo's words his color vanished, and a livid sheen took over his entire face and neck. Fargo was watching closely, saw the lips stretch into a hard, thin line, the eyes glitter, the big hands clench. The man, he saw, was fighting for control. Fargo remembered how the girl had told him of his jealousy and he had decided to play the card.

In the charged silence that followed Fargo's words, the door of the log house opened and Constance Bogardus stood in the doorway.

"Connie, a—uh—friend of yours is answering your invitation to visit . . . it appears." The words were metallic, shot like bullets from Bogardus's tight mouth.

Fargo was delighted at the success of his maneuver, and he was delighted to see that the girl in her sudden flame of anger at the outright lie appeared to be even more beautiful than before. But it was necessary to his game to drive a wedge between her and Bogardus, for whatever might happen.

At that moment he didn't know what to expect, but what he saw was a young woman with superb control in the face of a very difficult situation.

Constance Bogardus's smile was not at all glacial. It was almost warm as she said, "Well come in. Come in, Mr. Fargo. And Grady, I'm so glad you've finally met Fargo. He is, as Uncle Conrad said, tall, big, forceful, and not a little bit insolent. I'm sure you'll both hit it off beautifully!" And she turned on her heel, smiling even more warmly at both of them now, and disappeared into the house.

It was Fargo's turn to be surprised. But he didn't let himself get caught. Tearing his eyes from the girl, he watched Bogardus like a bear watching an anthill. The man was undergoing a severe inner upheaval: rage, jealousy, suspicion, impatience, and self-pity all fought to make up the expression in his face, in his tone of voice, as he said, "Good then, Fargo. Come on in. It's almost time for dinner. I hope you're hungry."

Although she had surprised him, Fargo could see that his plan was working. He had forced her into a fresh attitude toward him, and he'd put both of them on the defensive.

"Good enough," he said as he swung down from the Ovaro. And as one of the men approached to take the reins he said, "I'll put him in that round horse corral. Don't put anything in there with him." And he led the big black-and-white horse past the three young bays to the next corral.

When he got back to the log house, Constance Bogardus was at the door to greet him.

"It's a man's country out here," Bogardus was saying. "Not a country for tall boys called men." And his big, florid face creased in laughter at his own observation.

They had finished dinner and were seated around the table in the main room of the log house. Bogardus was smoking a cigar, and now Fargo joined him, lighting up as Constance poured three glasses of brandy.

"The good life," Bogardus said, "is what we're all after. I can see, Fargo, that you're a man who understands that philosophy."

Fargo nodded at his host. "I understand there've been a number of holdups in the country this past year," he said. He'd had the distinct feeling during the meal that Grady Bogardus had been avoiding any serious talk about his search for Uncle Jason, or about the outlawry that was rampant in and around the mining communities.

"More than a number," Constance said, chiming in. She looked at her husband, who was leaning back in his big overstuffed chair, gazing down at the toe on his Wellington boot.

"It's gotten pretty bad," Bogardus said. "Just as Connie indicates." His words were flecked with pessimism, which Fargo was quick to note.

The girl put down her glass of brandy. She was wearing a tight-fitting beige riding habit that showed off her superb figure. "I believe it has really taken a serious turn," she said. "The law doesn't seem able to do anything about it."

"Mostly stage holdups, I've heard," Fargo said mildly.

"That's right." Bogardus shifted his weight, sat up, cleared his throat. "No bank stuff." He leaned back with his elbows on the arms of his chair, his fingers arched together in front of him. "Tell me, though, how have you been doing? From the way you talk I gather you haven't had very much success in tracking down Uncle Jason." He nodded toward his wife. "Connie gave me details on your talk with Conrad. And I know you were at Piney Creek." He smiled suddenly. "My men told me."

131

"And I believe you were there too," Fargo speared suddenly at the girl.

She couldn't control the flush. "Yes, I was. As a matter of fact I thought I saw someone who looked like you, but I wasn't sure."

Fargo accepted the lame explanation of her not acknowledging his presence sooner.

"I ride over for supplies now and again when we're up here. We don't spend much time at the ranch. You know I do a lot of work for Conrad, and Grady is also part of the Six-Mile Company. The ranch, well it's mostly raising horses, riding, having a good time. It can almost run itself."

"With all those guns around?" Fargo suddenly speared at her.

"Good question, that," Bogardus came in with a little appreciative laugh. "You see, some of what we have is good racing stuff. Now you know with all the outlaws on the prowl smelling gold and silver, they'd love to have some of those fast horses."

"So you have your protection," the Trailsman said—and then he added, "Pretty smart." But he was really referring to the way Bogardus had handled the question of the hard cases in his employ.

Bogardus seemed to ease further into his big chair and now studied his guest with an attitude of complete composure. "I take it you haven't had much success in tracking down Jason," he said again.

"I wouldn't say that."

"Do you have some news then?" Constance's eyes were wide and bright as she turned them fully onto Fargo. "I mean we've been waiting all evening to hear some good news about Uncle Jason, but for myself I've simply assumed you didn't have any."

"One of those closemouthed westerners," Bogardus said with an amiable chuckle, and sat up in his big chair.

"Only a couple of straws in the wind."

"Enough straws you can build a haystack," said Grady Bogardus. "I think you're on to something, Fargo, but I'm not going to press you. You do realize, of course, that you've got the whole family on tenterhooks, waiting to see if you'll turn up Jason Rivers."

"I've got a pretty fair notion where he is," Fargo said, and he watched the surprise on the two faces as he stood up. "Want to thank you for the pleasant time."

Both Bogardus and his wife were on their feet. "But aren't you going to tell us what you've uncovered?"

"Too soon. And I could be wrong." And with a quiet smile the Trailsman started to the door.

"Is Uncle Jason anywhere near here?" Constance demanded. "Can't you tell us anything?"

"I don't have anything solid to tell, and anyway if I did, my agreement with Conrad, who is paying me, is that I tell him first." He put his hand on the door latch. Pausing, he said casually, "Always has interested me how a man who knows anything about horses knows them like the palm of his own hand; I mean, take these stage drivers, I am sure each one of them knows just about every horse around this part of the country."

"Sure you won't let us put you up for the night,

133

Fargo?" Bogardus was almost, but not quite, insistent.

"Thanks. I'll be heading toward the north fork of the Horsehead."

"To Jason?"

"Not much of a sure thing. And a good bit less than likely he might be about there." He opened the door and then said, "By the way. I only just found out that it was Jason discovered the Six-Mile, not his father."

"That is correct," Grady Bogardus said. "But of course, Daddy Rivers discovered the Ophir and all the rest of it."

"Just that it might explain why the old man left the whole shebang to Jason." And Fargo felt the distinct chill in the room as he stepped outside, closing the door behind him.

He walked warily out to the Ovaro, knowing how carefully he had to go now. He had pushed it as far as he could without coming out completely: the fast horses and the painting to change their markings, the stage drivers able to identify every fast horse in the country, the hint that he just might know where Jason Rivers was, and most of all, the impression that he knew a great deal more than he was telling. He hoped he hadn't overplayed it, but it was necessary to shake something loose.

It was dark, the stars dotting the sky, so numerous that it was almost a milky blanket overhead. Fargo had just put his hand on the gate of the round horse corral, had smelled the Ovaro, when he heard the step behind him.

"Fargo, I've got to talk to you."

He turned, catching the outline of her face as she looked up at him. "Go ahead."

"Be careful. Please be careful. That's all." And she started to turn away, but he reached out and held her.

In a moment she had moved against him and, raising her head, pressed her thighs against his. His rigid member drove like a club into her tight body.

"Fargo, I'm afraid!"

"Afraid of what?"

"I'm afraid of Grady. Please be careful." She pushed away from him. "I've got to go now. Please!"

Suddenly he drew her to him and pressed his mouth against hers. She remained rigid. With fear? he wondered. And then for just a second, something melted as her tongue slipped like a snake into his mouth, her legs parted to receive his thrusting organ, which was almost tearing his trousers. And then with a cry that was more a whimper, she broke from his grasp and ran to the house.

He rode quickly away from the ranch, puzzled more than ever by the strange girl, and stirred by the long-banked passion that she had revealed. He was not bothering to hide his tracks, but leaving a quite clear, though not obvious trail for the men he knew would be following him.

The Trailsman did not head for the copse of box elders where he had left Elbows McFowles. Instead he took a northern route not very far from the little stand of trees. He rode quickly at first, putting distance between himself and the Quarter Hitch, and then he slowed the big horse to a walk. After a while he knew they were behind him. It was the instinct he always had on the trail, which had always stood him in good stead, and which he attributed to his Cherokee blood.

Clearly, Grady Bogardus had gotten the message that the Trailsman knew more than he was telling, and he was worried. The pieces were beginning to fall more into a pattern, but still a pattern Fargo couldn't quite understand.

It was clear that the Quarter Hitch was somehow connected with the rash of stage holdups. There were the hard cases, there was the stage driver he'd recognized, and there were the fast horses and the painted markings. True enough, any man of the country, and especially a driver who knew horseflesh, would recognize an animal like he would one of his own family. The Quarter Hitch was the obvious hub of a stage-robbery operation. And it was clear that Grady Bogardus was at the center of it.

But what about Conrad Rivers? Was he in on it? And Constance? It seemed clear she was trying to warn him about something. But then she'd been with Fargo on the stage that was held up. It had been clear that the holdup men were planning to kill them all. Surely if Connie Bogardus was working with her husband on such an operation, a killing would have been out of the question. Answer: she was innocent, and hadn't been recognized.

Yes, he reflected. She could be quite innocent. But Bogardus was evidently mad about her, even though he did have his jollies elsewhere. Maybe

Connie was cold to his advances. In any case, it was plain to see that he was crazy for her and that she demanded much in the way of money and the good life. Bogardus wasn't a Rivers. He wasn't that rich. Maybe he'd had a rough time keeping his end up with Connie.

All these thoughts were running through his head when he crossed the little creek not very far from where he'd left Elbows some hours earlier. Presently he found the place he was looking for, a narrow passageway between two rock formations leading into a small meadow. Slipping the Sharps out of its saddle scabbard, he stepped down from the Ovaro, then wrapped the reins around the saddle horn and slapped the big horse on the rump, sending him into the meadow.

Quickly he started to climb up to a ledge just inside the opening of the two outgrowths of rock. He had just made it up to the place that overlooked the trail below when he heard the horses.

The moon had slipped into the sky now, and suddenly the land below was bright. Fargo had just made it up to the ledge in time. In a moment he saw the three riders approaching.

"He come down 'long here," said the man in the lead.

"Be careful, Joe. He's a smart sonofabitch and he could set us up. Them slabs of rock is pretty narrow."

The first speaker almost snarled his reply. "C'mon. Let's get shut of this and git on home." And he kicked his horse through the opening between the two big rocks. His companions followed suit.

They had just ridden slowly into the meadow when the man in front said, "There's that horse, but where the hell . . . !"

It was at that point that Fargo said, "Throw up your hands, the three of you. I mean right now!"

But the man in front had already struck for his handgun, another had dived out of the saddle, and the third bore testimony to the old saying that he who hesitates is lost as Fargo's Sharps cut him almost in half.

In a trice, the Trailsman had changed his position, dropping down from the ledge with his big Colt in his hand. For a second he saw the man who had been in the lead and felt the bullet whine past his head, followed by the crack of it. The Colt barked and the man who had fired doubled over, gut-shot.

The third man threw up his hands wildly. "Don't shoot! For God sake, don't shoot!"

Fargo wanted a prisoner, and he was glad he hadn't had to kill all three. Yet no sooner had the thought entered his mind than the other man streaked for a second weapon. But he rued the action, as the Trailsman's .45 barked just once, and the man fell, all but decapitated in a spill of blood.

Fargo, to his dismay, found that he had shot too well. The men were clearly beyond speech. Yet he didn't need any more proof. He knew they had come from the Quarter Hitch. His keen ears had picked them up on his back trail only minutes after he had left the Bogardus spread.

He found their bodies lying in the trail when

he rode back to where he had left the little old bronc stomper. Elbows was still alive, but not much more.

"Got the fuckers," he whistled as Fargo held his old gray head while the life ebbed swiftly out of him. "Dammit to hell, Fargo, I told you to leave me some booze. Those buggers would never've got me if I'd had some fortifier!"

"I'm sorry, old-timer," Fargo said gently. "I am sure sorry." He was about to reach for the bottle when he realized there was no need. Elbows McFowles was dead.

Fargo laid the small gray head down onto his rolled jacket, placing it there as carefully as he would have placed a very special jewel.

He slept little that night, his thoughts turning on the Rivers family and Uncle Jason. He had the feeling that he'd been missing something, something that was likely staring him in the face. Yet there were still those unanswered questions. Was Constance in on whatever Rivers and Bogardus were up to? It was clear now that the holdup operation was big, damn big, and therefore profitable. The horses the outlaws used were of course never recognized since any markings on them were painted over. Furthermore, it wasn't beyond the holdup men to simply kill all the stage passengers, including the driver and guard if they'd a mind to. Only why? Why was Bogardus into such an operation? And was Conrad Rivers with him? Did Connie Bogardus even know about it? Why had she warned him to be careful? And why was she afraid of her husband? Or was she lying, as part of some plan?

In the early morning he dug a shallow grave for Elbows McFowles and covered the little man's body with rocks so that animals would not disturb him. Halfway toward noon he rubbed down the Ovaro, curried him, then with a fresh determination he mounted up and rode south on his back trail. That evening he again found the place where the Shoshone woman had veered off toward the mountains. The sign was faint, and then vanished altogether as the trail grew into rock, and night fell. Fargo made camp, picketing the Ovaro, and ate a dry supper.

During the night a soft rain fell, and he knew that was the end of following the Indian's sign, at least for a while. In the morning, which broke bright and clear, he played a hunch and headed toward the river that he could hear in the distance. Presently, following a sharp turn in the trail, he rode around a large clump of chokecherry bushes, and there was the coursing river—the Pitchfork—small, but chock-full of water running over its banks.

Fargo walked the pinto into the rushing water, and while the horse stood cooling his feet and legs, the man eased himself in the saddle, squinting north toward the rim rocks and high mountains. He had that feeling he knew so well. It had to be in the mountains. What was more, the woman had been heading in that direction until her sign gave out.

He took off his big hat, ran his sleeve over his hot forehead, and put the hat back on again. It had to be that way. During the past few days he had been trying to work himself into the image, into the ways and movements of Jason Rivers—in short, to feel, to live the man. Who was Jason? What was he? He was sharp, obviously—witty, cynical, with a lot of feeling too, a good sense of humor, a man who could be counted on for one thing: the totally unexpected. This was the image Fargo had drawn from the conversation and his own perception. Jason didn't do things like ordinary people. He went on his own way. He could tell a billion dollars to go to hell. He could turn his back on his family and friends and go off and live with his Indian wife. He could go to San Francisco and wine and dine with the likes of Bill Ralston, or Jim Fair, or any of the other very rich and powerful, and he could live in a tipi town, or out in the real world too. Yes, decided Fargo, mostly out in the real world. And he made a dry camp while gray nightfall stalked the sky, the river, the breathing land.

Yes, he reasoned, a man such as Jason would find a place that was well away, well hidden, well protected. The Trailsman rode carefully along the eastern bank of the river as it wound north. Here and there he saw signs of passage and felt especially encouraged when he found a small ringlet of Indian beads: a Shoshone piece, obviously a woman's.

Yes, it made sense that she would come down for supplies. Jason would not wish to mingle with the people at Piney Creek. But who was the girl? Standing Eagle had indicated that Yellow Wing was dead, was it Singing Flower? Or was it someone else? Or—and this thought was not weak in him—was he perhaps on a wild-goose chase? Had

141

he read into the situation things that weren't really so? Maybe Jason Rivers wasn't even in the country!

He rested the Ovaro, taking time to eat some berries he had gathered along the trail, studied the high ridge on the other side of the river. He was sure that Jason would pick camp where the sun would not be in his eyes at any time. He would be protected by trees, rocks. There would be a spring. And the trail would be one that only an experienced woodsman could travel without making noises and so give himself away; it would be a trail with much of it visible from Jason's camp. In this manner, the Trailsman put himself into the shoes of the man he sought and finally found his eyes returning again to a place just below the high rim rocks across the river where it appeared as though some trees had been cut. The indentation along the line of the treetops was too regular in shape to have been caused by a storm. It was, in fact, quite unnatural. There would be pine and spruce up there, and he was just about certain that somebody had been felling them.

At noon he forded the river and started up the other side. For some distance the trail was open, visible from any direction, and it was steep. He simply followed it, reasoning that it would only be foolishness to try to hide, that such an attempt would only encourage suspicion from whoever was above.

He had dismounted and was now leading the Ovaro up the hard, twisting trail which ran through sage and hardpan. It was barely possible to see any tracks, and none that meant anything to him. But from the point of view of whoever might be living beneath the rim rocks, it was a perfect situation. An approaching rider or man on foot couldn't be more visible if he arrived with an army.

It was hot. Fargo was soon soaked through his shirt, and the headband of his big hat was limp with water. About midafternoon he reached the edge of the lower timberline, and now the going was easier. The air cooled perceptibly as the trail wound deep into spruce, pine, and fir, and the smell of the needles and cones mingled with the sage until finally overcoming it so that there was only the odor of the trees, the horse, and the man—and their silence. After a while the trail turned sharply and became softer; the ground at last turned mushy as Fargo heard the sound of water. It was an open spring he came upon, the water splashing lightly out of a crevice in some rock. He stopped to let the Ovaro drink and himself too, tasting long of the sweet mountain water, splashing it over his face, neck, and arms.

And yet at no moment was he without his attention. He had no notion if it was Jason's place he was coming to or somebody else's; nor, if it was Jason, how he would receive a visitor. He was taking a big chance coming in like this, he knew, for he was deliberately exposing himself in order to show that he came in peace. To do otherwise would have been to scare off his quarry or invite attack.

It was toward the end of the afternoon when he

rode the Ovaro across the little creek that edged the high meadow surrounded by pine and spruce.

The sunlight was spilling over the rich green grass as he drew rein. For some moments he sat the big horse, taking it all in. There was no sign of human life. At the far end of the little meadow he saw another spring, and now rode toward it, walking the pinto easily. From the spring he could see clear across the valley to the far rim rocks, and beyond them, north to the highest snowcapped mountains.

He sat there listening to the life of the meadow: the jays, the meadowlark who danced wildly in front of his eyes, the gentle sighing of the trees as a wind stirred them. The Trailsman was absolutely motionless as he sat the Ovaro, listening, feeling the life all around him and inside himself. It was a world here, a world within that other world of things and talk. He felt it in the throbbing of his blood, the coursing of his breath. As the sun began to leave the meadow, taking the warmth and gold behind the tall trees, he knew that he was being watched.

"Peaceful, ain't it?" said the grainy voice.

"It is that." Fargo didn't move. He remained as he was, alert to all his surroundings including the voice of the man in the trees behind him.

"Name is Skye Fargo," the Trailsman said, not changing his position on the Ovaro. "You're Flying Arrow, are you?"

"That is correct, young feller."

And Fargo heard the older man's breathing as he stepped out of the protection of the trees and walked around to stand in front of him.

"Have you et?" he said, looking up at his visitor.

"Always hungry," Fargo said easily, taking in the white-haired man with the broad shoulders, the bright aquamarine eyes, the long bony hands, one of which was holding a Hawkens plains rifle.

"You can picket the Ovaro," Jason Rivers said, "and I've got some tasty buffalo steak we'll make do with."

As he swung down from the big horse Fargo felt the bulge in his jacket pocket. "And I've got a drop of drink for you, Uncle Jason; a friend of mine left it for us just awhile back."

7

"Started the cabin awhile back," Jason was saying as he loaded his pipe. "Slow going now, getting the logs up, especially by myself." He chuckled inside his beard. "Not young like I used to be."

Fargo lit the cigar that his host had given him, leaned back against the saddle he'd taken from the Ovaro. It had been a full meal of buffalo hump, hominy, washed down with coffee, then followed by canned peaches. Jason had poured a second round of coffee, and Fargo had dealt out more whiskey from Elbows McFowles' bottle.

They were sitting in a second clearing, closer to the side of the mountain, and next to the little meadow where he had encountered Jason Rivers. The clearing was dominated by the half-built log cabin, about which Jason was presently speaking. It stood in the middle of the cleared ground, with an unobstructed view of the entire valley of the Pitchfork, including the great rim rocks on the far side, and beyond them the now shadowy mountains with their great shoulders slipping into the oncoming night. The sun was just down, but its light lingered, thrown up brilliantly from behind those far mountains of the West.

Fargo canted his head toward the work Jason had been engaged in. He had put up six courses of logs, which came to just higher than his head when he was standing. Now he was explaining to his visitor the difficulty of getting more logs up.

"Working by myself ain't what it used to be," he said wryly. "Could use some help lifting."

"I'd be obliged," the Trailsman said. "I've built some cabins in my day." He nodded toward the structure. "Always believed in coping instead of square cuts on the ends," he said.

Jason's long, guttered face creased in even more wrinkles. He was a handsome man, who stood and sat erect, with an easy mobility. There was something dignified about him, Fargo had immediately noted, yet nothing pompous. Now the old man said, "Coping's good so's the rainwater runs off and don't settle in the notches, I do agree. But see, I been working alone, and I'll be having to set up there on those walls and fit the logs. If I have to cope them to fit, then I got only the one ax and no adze, and the ax has got a long handle."

"Gotcha," Fargo said grinning. "And if you coped you'd want to cut the handle shorter so's you could use it while you're setting up there."

Jason nodded. "So I notch 'em square on the ground."

"Makes sense." Fargo nodded agreeably. "What are you figuring for chinking?"

"Some manure, but there isn't much about. Moss and wood strips mostly." The old man took the pipe out of his mouth, and spat down between his legs. He was sitting on a log, not far from the stack that was lying on a rack. He had told Fargo of cutting the trees the winter before and starting the cabin just after the last spring snow. For a long moment now he said nothing, and Fargo waited. They had had a quiet supper, Fargo not mentioning the purpose of his visit, and as the moments passed it became more evident that the time had come. Yet Fargo waited.

He waited, and he liked Jason Rivers. What he liked was the way the old man was appropriate to the moment. Like an Indian, Fargo was thinking. By God, ain't that a note! No wonder the family had trouble with him and he with them. Uncle Jason was his own man; he did things in his own time and in his own way.

"I have been looking for you, Uncle Jason," he said, using the family name intentionally; and he watched the light sweep into the older man's eyes.

"Thought so. I thought so. They hired you, eh?"

"Your brother Conrad hired me," Fargo said. "Your half brother, I believe."

A kind of chuckle came out of Jason's throat. With the back of his hand he wiped his mustache and beard, then put his pipe back in his mouth. "He'll be wanting something sure enough. What is it?"

"Your father is dead."

In the dying light, Jason turned his aquamarine eyes fully on his visitor. "About time, I guess. Pop would be at least ninety-five, going on a hundred."

There was something in the way he'd called his father "Pop" that told Fargo something. "You had a special way with him, I'd say."

Again, Uncle Jason waited for the moment to be right before speaking. And for Fargo it was good the way the silence built for a full minute. Then the old man said softly, but without any sentimentality at all. "He was a good man." And he added, "Only trouble was that asshole family. He couldn't get shut of them."

"But you did."

Jason nodded, tamping the bowl of his pipe with his thick middle finger. "I did." He sniffed, spat again down between his knees. "You know, it wasn't that so many of them, like Conrad and his two sisters, and Bogardus and some of the rest were so shitty, such liars and sniveling boobs, so goddamn dishonest, no . . . it was just that the whole bunch of them were just so goddamn dumb!" He paused. Only Melissa—Melissa was a free soul. You met her?"

"Oh yes!"

"And sometimes Connie—maybe Connie. Except she's married to that Bogardus."

After another long silence Fargo said, "They—and especially Conrad—want you to come back down to Virginia City and claim your inheritance. Melissa and Connie too."

"Inheritance?"

"It's a whole lot of money, they tell me."

"And they want me to come back and get it!"

"That is what they hired me for—to find you and tell you."

Jason's mouth, hidden behind his beard, had formed an O, his eyes had opened wide, forming two more large circles. There was a charged pause, and then with a sweep of both his hands flung high in the air, the old man broke into a crescendo of laughter. He roared, he shook, he almost fell off the log he was sitting on. He slapped his thighs, waved his arms in utter helplessness, while the tears poured down his face and he began to gasp for breath. For a moment Fargo feared he was having an attack. Finally he fell over backward and lay on the ground sucking air into his tearing lungs. He lay prone, crying with silent laughter now, while his old body began to regain it composure.

Jason's laughter was utterly contagious and Fargo had started to join him. The old man was like a child. Every part of his body laughed. But at length he fell silent, lying there on his back on the ground. And finally, they were both enveloped in silence.

Then suddenly, without any warning, Jason sat up. His face was dead serious, his voice even as a milled board as he said, "No. I am not going back. They can take the money and stick it you know where."

Fargo said nothing. There was nothing to say. Only, lying on his bedroll later that night, he knew that the matter was not ended with Jason's decision. He knew, just as he knew his own name, that Conrad and the members of the family who sided with him wouldn't be satisfied with Jason's go-to-hell reply. They'd want it in writing, they'd want it legal; from what Fargo could see they'd want it more than likely in Jason's death certificate. The only question was, he didn't know why.

In the morning he tried again. "Would you sign a paper giving them the money?"

"Mr. Fargo, I got to tell you I don't know how to

write anymore. I don't even know how to make a thumbprint like the Indians. You can tell Conrad and the rest of 'em to shove it. By God, I get pissed enough I'll just ride myself down there and take all that money!" He measured Fargo with his eye. "I like you; you're straight. Rare. You'll tell them the straight of it for me. I chose my life. I don't want that money, even though it was me found the Six-Mile and they all been living off it like kings and queens ever since. I don't want the money and I don't want that god-damn family. Now, sir, leave me be!" He had worked himself into a real anger. He was shaking, his mouth was quivering, and he kept clenching and unclenching his hands. He calmed a little now and turned his pale piercing eyes onto Fargo. "You tell 'em. I trust you. But get this, young man ..." And he held his forefinger out like a spike. "Don't never ask me that again. If you come back here, I'll have at you. Mind it, I can shoot the asshole out of a diving hawk, and you better know it."

"Good enough," Fargo said. But there was still some business not finished. Indeed, it hadn't even been mentioned. He waited though until he had saddled the Ovaro and was ready to mount.

"I know you don't live alone," he said suddenly, in a soft voice. "So you will have someone to help you with the cabin, that is, if they're about."

Jason had been studying the head of his ax as Fargo began to speak, testing it with his thumb to see it wasn't dulled. Without looking up he said, "I get some help for sure. But those spruce logs are heavy. It ain't work for a ... It's a man's work." And quickly he cocked his head at

151

the Trailsman who was standing next to the Ovaro. "You'll keep that to yourself, won't you, Fargo."

"All I know is you're not coming back."

The old man stood tall and straight as Fargo swung into the saddle. He looked down at Jason Rivers, standing there in the clearing with the half-built log house in back of him. "You've got plenty of ammo?"

"More being brought."

"They're not going to give up that easy. There's something more they want."

"I know. They can go to hell."

And Fargo caught the way the old man looked toward the opening at the other end of the clearing that led to the meadow and on back down the trail to the river. It was just a quick glance, but there was in it something that caught him— something secret.

Fargo leaned down, offering his hand, and Jason's grip was firm.

"Didn't want to take it out on you," he said.

"Just remember if I do come back, it'll be to help you finish the cabin." He reached into the pocket of his jacket, then and handed over what was left of Elbows McFowles' bottle. "From me and from its former owner," he said.

He turned the Ovaro and rode out of the clearing, out through the brilliant green meadow, and back down toward the river. His first destination would be Oroville.

Fargo watched her lips open, tremble, the tip of her tongue touch her upper lip as the dimples appeared at each corner of her wide mouth. Her lower lip moved out now, and he felt her breath on his face as he stood in front of her and began to unbutton her dress slowly. There was no sound in the wagon other than her breath, which grew louder, quicker, and then the tight gasp as her big breasts burst out of her clothing.

They were cool, the nipples large, firm to his finger and his tongue as he bent down and took one into his mouth, bit on it gently. Her moan ran through her entire body as her dress swept to the floor, and now his hands slipped into her pants, pushed them down below her knees, pressed his rigid member into the black forest of soaking desire between her silken legs.

Aphrodite pulled him on top of her as she fell back onto her bed, the two of them tearing off his clothes until that exquisite moment when they were both totally naked.

"God, oh my God, Fargo. Quick! Please—quick!" And then she was heaving beneath him, her long legs gripping around his pumping buttocks as he thrust into her high and deep, dragging the moaning out of her, the muffled screams of delight.

Fargo felt the spasms rippling through her as her body pumped with his, and when he suddenly withdrew she cried out, "Oh my God, no— Fargo, please! Dear God, Fargo, don't stop!"

But he had spun her over onto her hands and knees and had now entered her soaking lips from the rear, riding her high, thrusting her up into the air. Her voice was muffled in the bedclothes as he rode her side to side, in and out, and then in changing circles.

"My God, faster ... faster!" Her cries swept through the wagon until the moment when—

riding her almost right through the bed, so strong was the thrusting and squirming—he came, shooting her with his hose as she climaxed in total response.

Slowly she turned onto her back and again began to undulate, this time bringing his member into an even greater rigidity until once more they burst together, locked in each other's thrashing arms and legs, while he gripped her pounding buttocks and she dug her fingernails into his back.

They lay gasping and exhausted in their heated, soaking satiation.

"Far-go," she said in her Spanish accent. "How *far* you *go*—inside me! God!"

He grinned up at the top of the wagon. "And you, Aphrodite. You know your name all right: goddess of love."

"I am glad you came back to see Aphrodite. I will read your fortune—for free."

"You don't have to."

"I want to do something nice for you."

"You just did."

"You want more?"

"Sure."

She was silent a moment and they lay side by side in her bed, looking up at the top of the wagon.

"Fargo—you do it with Candy?"

"That ain't any of your business," he said, leaning up on an elbow."

"Wait!" Her fingers touched his arm. "I am not jealous. I wonder if you like to do it with me and Candy both some time." And her laugh tickled his ear as he lay back down beside her.

154

"I'll give it some thought," he said. "But right now it's getting late and I've got some things to do."

"Maybe you come later."

"I'll come anytime you like, honey."

He had sat up and swung his legs to the floor; she stayed on her back, running her fingers along his arm.

"Where do you go?"

He turned and looked at her. "You know something? You ask too damn many questions. When I'm with you, I'll be with you; and when I'm not, I'm not."

Suddenly she raised herself up on her elbow and then bent to his crotch and kissed him. "Just remember," she said, talking to his organ. "Aphrodite waits for you. Aphrodite loves you."

"You make it hard for me to leave," he said, standing up.

"Yes—yes. I want to make him hard—again and again and again and again . . ."

"Just so long as you make him soft in between times," he said, pulling on his trousers.

And in a moment he slipped out of the wagon into the dark night that encompassed Oroville, the hamlet that comprised the Six-Mile Mine and the Ophir and the Red Jacket and the Quad.

He had ridden in after dark—unnoticed by anyone, as he had planned—and had camped not far from an abandoned mine shaft. Although it was night, there had been enough light from the moon to see his way about, and he had made out the medicine show and circus wagons instantly, plus the dilapidated shacks near the mine openings, and some other buildings. Oro certainly agreed with the description Melissa had given. There was nothing here except mines—many of them abandoned—and the people who worked them.

He had encountered Aphrodite quite easily when he'd seen the door of her wagon open and Candy O'Hara come out and walk toward her own wagon. Being careful not to run into anyone, he walked quickly to the wagon, hoping to find out any gossip that might help him, or anything else that would indicate why the circus had come to such a deserted place as Oro. But the only news she had was that they were pulling out the following evening; she didn't know where.

He then walked over to where he had left the Ovaro and his gear.

He had just spread his bedroll when he heard the horses, two of them riding in fast. They pulled up in front of Candy O'Hara's wagon, the wagon with the singing wheels. Fargo couldn't tell if they were from the Quarter Hitch. Even with the moon out, they were obscured by some bushes which lay between him and the wagon. But he could see they were hurried: the horses were blowing; the steps of the men and the rap on the door of the circus wagon were impatient.

Light spilled through the door as Candy opened it, stood framed, and then stepped back to allow the two visitors to enter.

Fargo moved closer, careful to keep out of sight of anyone who might be wandering around. It wasn't late and there were lights on in the circus wagons and in some of the shacks that he guessed housed the miners.

He had moved close to the two horses to see if

he could recognize them; he'd a strong notion the men had indeed ridden over from Piney Creek. But he had no chance for a close examination. The door of the wagon suddenly opened and the two men emerged.

"You can take that second cabin," Candy was saying as they stepped outside. Fargo could not see her.

"See you in the morning then," one of the men said. And the other one added, "Early. Real early."

Fargo heard Candy O'Hara mumble something and then, more clearly, the word, "Can't see the big hurry. Shit, we just got here."

"That is the orders," one of the men said. "From Mr. Rivers."

"He is here?" There was rude surprise in the girl's voice.

"At Piney. And he wants the wagons over there fast."

The door closed, and Fargo waited while the two led their horses over to the shack indicated by the girl.

He waited a few minutes more and then began examining the ground the wagon was standing on, noting right away that there were hardly any indentations in the soil from the big wheels, yet remembering clearly the deep ruts at Piney Creek. Now, casting caution aside, he backtracked the imprints of the wagon wheels. The moon helped. At the same time, he himself was more visible should someone come out of one of the wagons or shacks. But he knew he couldn't wait till morning when people would be about and whatever tracks there were could be easily obliterated.

He was lucky. He was able to follow the wagon

tracks back to one of the mine openings. But he didn't go all the way to the mine shaft for fear a guard might be on duty.

Again he took a chance, after waiting a good while with no one appearing, and stepped over to the shaft and examined the ground right at the entrance. The ruts were deeper, even though the consistency of the ground was much the same as where Candy's wagon was now standing with hardly any marks under the wheels.

He was just about to step inside the shaft when he heard steps coming from behind him. In a flash he ducked into an outhouse. Through a crack in the door he saw a man appear, calling out "Hank—you there?"

A muffled voice came from within the mine. "Yo!"

"Coffee. Come on over."

Fargo listened to the receding steps, then entered the mine. He calculated he had maybe five minutes, for, depending on how strict the security, the guard would be right back with his coffee or he might remain to drink it with his companion. In either case, it was necessary to work fast.

There was just enough light for him to see. Inspecting his surroundings, he found that he was actually in an abandoned stamp mill. And then he saw what he was really looking for: a stack of silver bullion on top of some timbers at one side of the enclosure, and beside the stack four heavy canvas sacks of what in a moment he discovered to be gold coin. Three of the sacks were from merchants in Virginia City, being sent to San Francisco for deposit in their banks. The fourth was from the Ace and Player.

He stood there for a moment while it all clicked into place. The loot was stolen from the Wells, Fargo stages, the bullion then melted down, then recast in a new mold and explained as products of the Six-Mile ore. Neat. Candy O'Hara's medicine show and circus was used to transport the loot from the Quarter Hitch to the "mine." And it explained the desperate search for Uncle Jason. If Conrad Rivers was in the outlaw business, it must mean the Six-Mile had run dry. And with the railroad coming in, the holdup operation would be done for. Uncle Jason was the one and only answer—or rather his money was.

Suddenly he heard voices, and he snuffed the candle.

"Thought I saw a light!"

"Better leave off the tarantula juice," another voice said with a laugh as steps approached at the mouth of the shaft.

Fargo had drawn back into a far corner behind some fallen timbers. He waited for any light that might appear, but after a few curses one pair of footsteps receded, and the other clomped out toward the outhouse.

In a moment Fargo had stepped outside and moved quickly to where he had left the Ovaro and his bedroll. In minutes he had mounted the big black-and-white horse and was on his way to Piney Creek.

There was still one thing missing, and it had been nagging at him ever since he had ridden away from Jason Rivers and his half-built log cabin. It had been the way the old man had cut his eye not once but, he now remembered, twice toward the trail leading out of the clearing and on down to the river. And he was cursing himself now for not having realized the importance of those brief glances. He had thought that the Indian woman—was it Singing Flower?—had just been staying away while he visited, keeping out of sight the way Indian women were trained to do. But the look in the old man's eyes when he had glanced toward the trail should have told him differently. Singing Flower, or whoever it was, had not yet returned from Piney Creek trading post, and she'd had a good head start on him, plenty of time to get there. He had wrongly assumed she would have come from a different direction to cover her tracks. But the old man's look said no. And she wouldn't have gotten lost. That left only one other thing that could have happened to her.

8

It was clear to him now why Singing Flower hadn't returned from Piney Creek. The Quarter Hitch men had found out who she was. It had to have been a chance remark, something she'd said while buying her supplies. They had told Rivers at once, and he'd seized the opportunity to take the girl as bait. Fargo rode the pinto swiftly now, his anger capped by prudence. He knew he had to act fast, very fast, and without any mistake.

By now Jason would be looking for Singing Flower. He would realize what had happened, and would come in. Probably Conrad—and it must be Conrad, and likely Bogardus too, behind the capture of the girl—would not do anything rash, such as violently holding her. He would simply use her as a card in the game, a highly important card. And Jason would come for her. Fargo had no proof yet he knew it was the only way the game was being played. And he knew too that Conrad's plans did not include Jason's making it to Piney Creek.

He rode all through the rest of the night, stopping only when he felt it necessary to rest the

Ovaro. With luck, Jason might have waited a little longer for the girl to show up. But Fargo remembered the look on the old man's face. No, he would have left soon after he himself had left, probably that same day, or night.

Fargo made good time; the Ovaro was strong and steady. He knew the gunmen would be sent from the Quarter Hitch and so he didn't waste time riding to Piney but cut right across the high country and then dropped down at Whiskey Creek, following the line of willows until he reached the Pitchfork at Stinking Water Crossing. From there, as the sun rose swiftly into the sky, he rode toward the still-distant rim rocks from which he knew Jason Rivers would have come.

The Quarter Hitch men, he figured, caught her on the tableland just above the place where the girl's tracks had disappeared in rock after she had left Piney Creek with her sack of supplies. And those men who would go out now for Jason would be spotted at various points along the trail—to bushwhack him one way or another. The problem for the Trailsman was to figure which way Jason would come.

More than likely, Jason would know the trail Singing Flower had taken. He would have warned her to be careful, but he would trust her blood. He would know that she could handle herself as far as nature went. But about men, men bent on doing harm, that was another matter.

So Jason would follow her trail. As he rode, the Trailsman visualized Jason's moves. He would be afoot, for there'd been no horse, at least that he had seen. And he would be reading sign. Yet he would be suspicious after hearing about Conrad and the family. At some point he would cut away from the trail and probably move along parallel to it, or possibly take shortcuts provided he knew the country that well. Which Fargo was counting on. It meant that Jason would try and cut the girl's trail at strategic points, looking for her, not following the trail directly.

Decided on his plan, Fargo headed straight for a second crossing of the Pitchfork where it doubled back about three miles north of Stinking Water Crossing. It was a place he had taken note of when he first rode up to Jason's cabin. Well protected with thick clumps of box elders and willow, it offered a clear view of all approaches. If his hunch and his calculation were right, he would stand a good chance of getting to Jason first.

He had just rounded a cutbank a few hundred yards to the south of the crossing when he heard the crack of a rifle. He dug heels into the big horse, who sprang into a gallop. As he bore down on the three men who were firing at someone in the willows, he drew out the Sharps and, finding an even balance on the racing pinto, fired. It was enough. He had aimed at the man in the center of the three, but just as he pulled the trigger the man on the right moved over, and Fargo's bullet killed the first man, then went on to deliver a glancing wound to the second, who immediately threw up his arms. The third man dropped his rifle and fell flat on his face. Meanwhile, as Fargo pulled the Ovaro to a stop with his gun on the two still-living Quarter Hitch men, Jason Rivers walked out of the big clump of willows.

"Good shooting there, Fargo," he said. "Bastards jumped me unexpected."

"That's what I know. And there will be a couple or so more little greeting parties just like them."

"What are the bastards shooting at me for?" the old man demanded. He was clearly shaken, but not afraid. Not a bit afraid, Fargo could plainly see.

"I'll explain that while we head for Piney." He looked down at the two would-be bushwhackers. "First strip their guns, throw 'em in the river, 'less you want one."

"What you gonna do with us?" the man who had been creased along the cheek asked.

Fargo looked at him and at his companion, who had risen to his knees. "Get up," he said. "You can start walking. Next time I see you I'll kill you." He paused, slipping the Sharps into its saddle holster. "That is not a threat; it's a promise." He turned to Jason. "Climb on one of them ponies; we'll lead the other two."

One of the two, the one who hadn't been wounded, raised enough courage to snarl, "You bastard, Fargo!"

The Trailsman leaned forward onto the pommel of his stock saddle. His words were as hard as bullets. "That's right. And you just remember that."

In another few minutes he had ridden away, leading the two saddle horses, Jason on the third.

That night they camped near another turn of the river, ate a dry supper, and spelled each other on lookout.

"How friendly are you with Standing Eagle?" Fargo asked Jason as the old man was loading his pipe.

"He is my father-in-law. He approved of me."

"He says he wants to see his granddaughter."

"So do I." And the old man's milky eyes looked into the distance.

"Think Standing Eagle might want to help you find her?"

"I dunno. It could be him who took her."

"That crossed my mind," Fargo said. "Only I don't think so."

"Could be some of his young men, trying to look good."

"What if you were to pay him a visit. You'd likely have been doing that sooner or later anyway, wouldn't you?"

"It'd be the right thing to do. Only thing is, I got to find her. Standing Eagle's camp isn't all that close. I don't mind telling you I am worried, Fargo. For her. She's just a young girl. Those bastards. Hell, you know what they're like. I've got to get to her; I mean fast!"

"I know what they're like. But I want you hiding out."

"And Singing Flower?"

"If she's alive, I'll find her. I'll find her even if she isn't. That is a promise. But I know she is alive."

Riding toward the creek, past the low butte and in full view of the Quarter Hitch ranch houses, he knew he could be picked off easy as swatting a deerfly. But it was the time for boldness and he was also counting on Rivers' curiosity.

They would see he didn't have Jason, but they would not yet know about the three men at the Stinking Water Crossing, nor that Jason had eluded any other outriders. And so Conrad Rivers would be curious.

Now the sun was up and he could feel it on his back, and when he leaned forward, on the back of his neck. His eye caught a rider off to his left just slipping down into a draw, while to his right another was briefly outlined. When he reached the box elders and dropped from sight of the Quarter Hitch ranch house, he felt himself loosen all over. Not that he had been tense, but it had been a long ride and he had stayed in the saddle all the way. Now he felt really loose and in a good way; for the action was about to begin. He lifted the gait of the Ovaro, rode up a shallow draw, and came suddenly right onto the main house. He could feel the eyes on him as he sat the big horse, waiting.

Suddenly the big door opened and Conrad Rivers stepped out onto the big flat rock that served as a doorstep. "Why Fargo! What a surprise! I hope you bring good news."

Right behind him Grady Bogardus appeared, also with surprise in his face. "So you've taken us up on our invitation for a return visit."

Fargo had swung off the Ovaro and now walked toward the two men.

"Well, is it good news?" Rivers repeated, his face shining with his question.

"I'd say good."

"Come on inside. It's near dinner time. How about something? I'll bet you're hungry as a bobcat." Rivers' hand swept him to a chair. "Grady, may I apologize for taking over your role of host, but I'm so glad to see Fargo."

Bogardus's face was cut in a tight smile, and Fargo had a good view of the relationship between the two men. Grady now left the room, saying he was bringing whiskey and some glasses. Fargo and Rivers seated themselves, the latter instantly offering a cigar and taking one himself. "You remember this good smoke, I hope."

"I sure do," Fargo said, biting the little bullet of tobacco off the end and accepting Rivers' light. When Bogardus returned with three glasses and a bottle of whiskey, Fargo said, "You want news?"

A flash of irritation suddenly cut through Rivers' face, but he smiled quickly to cover. "But of course. It's been a long time. You've found Uncle Jason?"

And suddenly, through a second door, Connie Bogardus swept in. "Oh, I couldn't help overhearing! You have found him? Is it true?"

"It's true," Fargo said, his eyes falling pleasurably onto her eager face. He had never seen her quite so alive. It was a delightful shock and awakened his desire even more.

"Well, now, Fargo. Don't keep us in any more suspense," Grady Bogardus said. "Where is Jason?"

"He's right close. He is hale and hearty."

Rivers leaned forward, his elbows on his knees, drink in one hand, cigar in the other. "What do you mean, near here? Where is he—actually?"

"He's all right, in safe hands." Fargo took a pull at his drink, milking the moment to catch the nuances of their different reactions. "There's just one bit of business that we have to attend to first."

Rivers got the message right away. He turned

to Connie. "Connie, would you excuse us? I need those papers copied, you know the ones dealing with Jason and the back expenses of the Six-Mile."

"Do I have to do that now?"

"I wish you would."

"Very well." She stood up. Fargo could see she didn't like it, but it told him something he wanted to know—that she'd had nothing to do with Singing Flower. It was difficult for him to keep his eyes from her as she left the room, the very slight odor of hyacinth lingering as the door closed.

Conrad Rivers' face was a mask as he turned now to Fargo. "What is it then?"

"I believe you know already. Singing Flower."

Rivers cut his eyes quickly at Grady Bogardus. Both of Fargo's hosts were sitting in easy chairs, while he had chosen a straight, low-backed wooden chair, from which he would be able to draw his gun easily if he had to. When he saw Rivers' eyes snap to his holstered Colt, he knew the other man realized it too.

"What about Singing Flower? She is safe, well. No one has harmed her. I—we simply offered her hospitality until her—uh—father decided to come and see us. To see me," Rivers amended quickly, and cleared his throat. "My little plan worked, as you can see. Now there's no reason why she can't leave."

"Good. I'll take her with me then," Fargo said, and stood up.

Rivers and Bogardus both rose to face him.

Conrad Rivers took the cigar out of his mouth. "I want to see my brother."

Fargo nodded. "Why not?" He walked to the door of the room, out to the little hallway, and opened the front door. "Come on outside," he called over his shoulder. And he drew his six-gun and, raising it over his head, fired once.

Almost immediately men came running from the bunkhouse where they had gathered for the noon meal. Fargo still had the .45 in his hand.

"Tell them to calm down," he said. "Just telling Jason to ride on in."

Rivers waved his hand at the men and now, standing next to Bogardus, he looked in the direction of Fargo's gaze. Neither Bogardus nor Rivers noticed that Connie had joined them, but Fargo had again smelled the hyacinth. He didn't turn his head; he kept watching along the slow rise of land that led up to the timberline, and in a moment he saw Jason Rivers appear on the horse of one of the outlaws he had shot up at the river crossing.

"It is him," Bogardus said, and Fargo watched his eyes sweep to the knot of Quarter Hitch men who stood several feet away.

A trace of a smile touched the Trailsman's mouth. "It might interest you two fellows to know—and also your boys yonder—that right behind Jason in that timber is Standing Eagle and fifty Shoshone warriors. Standing Eagle is Jason's father-in-law—using white-man terms—and anyway, more important, he is Singing Flower's grandfather. You get my drift?"

Rivers had turned white under his smooth skin. "I find that hard to believe, Fargo. Jason is a white man. Not a goddamn Injun!"

"He was married to an Indian. And his child is Indian, since the Indians go by the mother's line, not the father's."

"You're bluffing. I don't see any Indians."

"He is bluffing, Conrad," Bogardus said.

"There's a way to find out. And while you're at it, you can find out if this .45 pointing right at your guts is bluffing, Rivers." Fargo grinned. "Take your choice."

Jason had been walking his bay horse slowly toward them. There was still no sign of Indians that either Rivers or Bogardus could see.

Fargo called out, "You men unbuckle. Right now!"

Rivers opened his mouth to say something, but he was like a fish gasping in the fresh air. "Very well," he said finally. "Grady . . ." But his eyes were still scanning the line of trees.

"Now Grady, go get the girl!" Fargo said, his eyes on the Quarter Hitch gunmen dropping their guns.

"The girl!" Bogardus looked dumbfounded, stalled at the turn of events.

"Singing Flower, you fool!" snapped Rivers.

"Singing Flower?" It was Connie's turn to be surprised. "Who is Singing Flower?"

"She is one of your latest relatives," Fargo said with a tight smile, his eyes on the approaching rider.

But now Constance Bogardus had seen who the old man on the horse was and she called out, "Uncle Jason!"

"Don't go out there!" Fargo said as he felt her move. "Stay right here."

Another moment passed and he felt that something was going to break. Maybe Jason was taking too long, but he could feel the rage and frustration in the man standing before him. Conrad Rivers was gray, sweating, in the mood to kill. The man, Fargo realized, was looking at a fortune riding toward him, a fortune that could have been his. That—but for fate or luck or something—could still be his!

"I still do not see any Indians out there, Fargo," Rivers said, regaining some of his composure.

Out of the side of his eyes Fargo saw Bogardus's arm move. He wheeled, firing the Colt, and Grady Bogardus fell twisting to the ground, gripping his gun arm where Fargo's bullet had shattered the bone.

Meanwhile, some of the gunmen had dived for their weapons and opened fire on Jason. But the old man had his Hawkens up and drilled two of the Quarter Hitch men before succumbing to a bullet in his rib cage that knocked him off the horse.

Fargo, spinning, fired once, twice—hitting one man in the chest, the other in the throat. The remaining gunmen dropped the weapons and froze.

"Drop it, Fargo!"

He turned to face Conrad Rivers' small but potent derringer.

"I said—drop it!"

Fargo lowered his gun slowly.

"Connie, stay where you are!" The girl had started to run toward Jason. "Tend to your husband, woman!"

He had not taken his eyes off Fargo for even a split second. "I said—drop your gun! I want it down on the ground—at your feet!"

Fargo let the .45 fall, the heavy piece of metal landing right on top of his foot.

There was a smirk all over Rivers' face as he

faced the Trailsman now. "You were bluffing all along, but I wasn't fooled."

"They were just a little late getting here," Fargo said easily. "But take a look behind you."

"I won't fall for that old turkey. What do you take me for!"

"Maybe you won't fall for a turkey, but you'll sure enough fall for a slug between your shoulder blades," Fargo said, and he let his eyes move past the man standing in front of him with the derringer pointed right at his chest.

Fargo watched the change in Rivers' breathing; he was waiting for something in the other man's eyes as he said, "You're through Rivers. The holdup game is finished. The mines'll be shipping by railroad before you know it, using sealed boxcars. It won't be like holding up a stagecoach."

"That's precisely why the money from Daddy will be so welcome and—uh—necessary. I didn't count on you being so damn nosy, Fargo. I had hoped you'd have the good sense to find Jason for me; nothing more."

"Not my style, Rivers."

"I'll even save a little money on not having to pay you." He grinned. "Every little bit helps."

Fargo's eyes slipped past the other man as he said, "They are right there, Rivers. You're not going to look pretty after Standing Eagle gets through with you. He doesn't appreciate your stealing his granddaughter."

Suddenly Rivers' eyes flicked and he shouted, "You men behind me! Are there Indians up on that hill!"

It was the split second Fargo had been waiting for, when Rivers' attention would be divided between himself, his men, and the possibility of Indians at his back. He felt the weight of his .45 on his foot, knew it was balanced. And swift as the flick of an eye he kicked the heavy gun into the other man's shins. In that same second he twisted, ducked, and brought a chopping punch down on Rivers' gun hand. He heard the bones crack as the derringer fired, the bullet flying harmlessly into the air. In the next moment he had retrieved the .45 and had everyone covered.

"Connie, check Uncle Jason. Your husband's only wounded." He looked down at Rivers, who was twisting in pain from his smashed shinbone but even more from his broken wrist.

The girl had raced out to her grandfather, who was now sitting up. "Just creased me," he called out. The fall from the horse was worse than the bullet. And now he was walking in, his arm around the girl.

"Damn you, Fargo!" snarled Rivers, who had finally managed to get to his feet. "You were bluffing! I knew there weren't any Indians, you lying sonofabitch!"

The grin on Fargo's face was an innocent as a mountain pond.

"So? Then you were right about something, Rivers. You were right that I was bluffing."

The night was warm and he stretched out on his bedroll, letting himself relax fully. Thank God it was over. But everything had ended well, he reflected, picturing Jason's great joy at being reunited with his daughter. The old man had almost broken down and cried, but then had turned

173

to laughing, and then, not knowing which to do, had finally done both.

Connie had taken care of both Conrad and her husband, neither of whom was seriously wounded.

"What will happen now?" she had asked Fargo.

"That's up to Uncle Jason. He can prosecute them, or he can do what he's always done—walk away. I'm out of it." He paused, taking in her much softer look as she stood facing him where he had been rubbing down the Ovaro. "I have one question," he said.

"What is it?"

"Why did you follow me out that day I met Rivers, and why did you want to see what was going into that Wells, Fargo stage?"

"I was following Conrad's orders about the stage. I didn't know why he wanted that information, but I was working for him. And as far as talking with you, I . . ." Her eyes looked suddenly at his mouth. "I just felt like it."

He grinned, suddenly liking her. "Good. That's the best reason I've heard for anyone doing anything since I took on this crazy assignment."

She ducked her head a little as she reached into a bag she was carrying. "I want to give you your pay," she said, handing him an envelope.

"Thanks. And is there any bonus?"

He watched the color sweep into her cheeks, and he thought she looked adorable.

"You could look in the envelope," she said, and turned on her heel and walked quickly toward the house.

He was thinking of how she looked, now as he lay on his bedroll looking up at the darkening sky. Something had changed in her. Had she grown up? People did, even when they got quite old, he knew. And he thought fleetingly of Elbows McFowles.

He sighed suddenly, not feeling sleepy, yet tired. He would miss Melissa, and he wondered what Jason would do about Candy and the medicine show. How much involved they all were he wasn't sure. What the hell, you had to make a living in this world. And for a moment his thoughts turned appreciatively to the talents of Candy O'Hara and the magnificent Aphrodite.

He had just closed his eyes when he heard the steps approaching up the short trail to where he had made his camp.

"You're late," he said as she came out of the long dark shadows of the trees. "But I forgive you. The stars are out in celebration."

"Is it all right?" she asked. "The note was all right?"

He felt her nervousness as she stood looking down at him. She was wearing the riding habit he especially liked, with the low-cut silk blouse and tight britches.

"What note?" he asked in surprise. And then he remembered the envelope with his money in it.

"You didn't open the envelope," she chided.

"What did the note say?"

"I forget now."

He reached up and took her hand, half raised himself, and drew her down beside him. "I've been waiting," he said.

"And so have I. Oh my God, dear Fargo, so have I."

And it was as though neither one decided

anything, but the life in one needed the life in the other as their lips met. Her lips opened wider and her tongue darted into his mouth, curled, asking. His hands began to feel over her, along the smooth line of her buttocks and thighs, then his fingers began undoing her britches.

"Oh, Fargo, Fargo—it's taking so long. But take your time, only not too long." And she was undulating her body as he undressed her, and she him.

Now his hands slipped over her warm, soft flesh, and he drew her flat onto the bedroll, pressing his head into firm, upturned breasts. She cried out, holding one breast for his mouth. Then he took the other, sucking, caressing. And at last his hand slid down her body and found her brush as she gasped and her legs began to open and close in quick, eager movements.

She was on her back now, her legs spread, her nails digging into his buttocks as he lowered himself, and then reaching down she grasped his organ, bringing it into the wet, furry slit.

"Yes, yes, yes, Fargo . . . Oh, my God, Fargo . . . Aaaaiiiii . . ." she screamed as his fingers explored all the crevices of her pulsing body. His fingers slid all over her, finding the secret places of the most exquisite desire, the greatest hunger and need, while she clung to him, pushing, and rolling her throbbing hips against him, taking in all the inches of him in the tightest embrace, while she cried for more and more and more. . . .

Until at last the moment of highest ecstasy was totally unbearable and he drove his great thrusting stick down and up into her pounding and squirming and hugging and tight, wet, racing orifice of paradise. They exploded together, having worked themselves halfway down the little hill to lie in ecstatic exhaustion on a bed of pine needles.

Later, after they had slept and awakened in the soft, bright moonlight, she whispered in his ear. "I hope the bonus was all right."

"Ah, the note . . ."

"It said, could I come and talk to you about what had happened."

"I'll turn it over," he said, whispering back to her ear.

She raised her head, looked at him. "Think it over?"

"There's nothing to talk about. You've got Jason back. And Melissa. I guess she'll be happy about it. As for Rivers and Grady, they're big boys, they'll just have to grow up."

"And what about Connie?" she asked, pretending to sulk.

"If Connie is a good girl, she can ride with me as far as Virginia City. Of course that might take awhile."

"And what if she isn't a good girl?" she asked, burying her happy laughter in his ear.

"Then she'll just have to ride with me to Virginia City," he said, "and that might take an even longer while."

LOOKING FORWARD

**The following is the opening section
from the next novel in the exciting new
Trailsman series from Signet:**

THE TRAILSMAN #24:
TWISTED NOOSE

*Idaho, in the early 1860s,
when it was still part of the Oregon Territory,
just west of the Bitterroot Range . . .*

He had only two days.

Two days for an almost three-day ride.

Two days to stop them from hanging Nellie Noonan.

The grim facts stabbed at the big man with the lake-blue eyes and the intense, chiseled face. Two days and it wasn't going well and now these two stupid bastards were trying to give him trouble. He cursed inwardly. The Ovaro had cracked a shoe on a rock and that's why he was at the blacksmith's in this dust-ridden little town with no name, really hardly more than a way station. He'd left the horse with the blacksmith, gone to get a cup of coffee, and the two men had been in the smithy's when he'd returned.

"I told you, the horse isn't for sale," Fargo said

again, lifting his voice above the pounding of the smithy.

"We made a fair offer, mister," one of the men said. "When we make an offer, you take it." He left the rest of the threat hanging in a caricature of a smile.

The big man's lake-blue eyes narrowed at the two men. They were cheap drifters, mean-mouthed, gimlet-eyed. He had no time for trouble, no time to risk their getting lucky, no time to haggle with them. He raised his voice again as the blacksmith continued to pound a shoe on his anvil. "Get out of here or you're both dead men," he said.

"You threatening us?" the other said with a sneer.

"I'm promising," Skye Fargo snapped back. He watched the two men exchange arrogant glances as the smithy's anvil continued to resound with ear-splitting blows. His hand was poised to whip the big Colt .45 from its holster when the blow came from behind. He felt the sharp explosion of pain as the butt end of a six-gun smashed into the back of his head, felt his legs turn to water and the curtain of blackness sweep over him. He was unconscious as he hit the stone floor of the blacksmith shop.

Sensations, wet, cold, a stab of pain ... they flicked finally inside him, told him he was alive. He forced his eyes open as another splash of cold water hit his face. He blinked, focused, and the figure before him took shape, became the blacksmith. The man's angular face peered down at him with concern and Fargo pushed himself up on one elbow, winced at the pain in the back of his head. The blacksmith pushed a wet towel at him. "Here, press this on your head," the man said.

Fargo took the towel, reached one big hand up and back and held the wet cloth to the throbbing spot on his head. His eyes swept the shop with instant apprehension and the smithy answered his gaze.

"They took the Ovaro," he said.

"Sons of bitches," Fargo muttered as he pushed himself to his feet. His mind raced as he put together what had happened. "How many were there?" he asked.

"Three," the blacksmith said.

Fargo's eyes bored into the man. "They had you pound that anvil so I wouldn't hear the third one sneaking up behind me," he said.

The smithy nodded, his eyes filled with apology. "I couldn't help it. They told me they'd blow my head off if I didn't stay at the anvil," he said. "They must've seen you come in with your horse because they showed up right after you went for coffee."

Fargo's oath stayed inside him as he saw more precious hours slipping away. "I want a horse," he said to the smithy. The man nodded. "I won't have time to bring him back," Fargo added.

"I'll give you the old bay," the man said. "He'll find his way back." Fargo's hand went to the holster and he swore again as he touched only emptiness. The blacksmith nodded. "The one that bushwhacked you took it, short little weasel with a tan vest. I've only my own gun. I can't give you that."

"Just get the horse," Fargo bit out. He walked to the doorway of the shop, his eyes following the hoof prints in the ground. They led northwest. At least it was in the right direction, he grunted bitterly. The smithy appeared with the old bay, a sturdy horse with legs still good, Fargo saw in one practiced glance.

"The Ovaro's got a good new shoe on," the smithy said, and Fargo started to reach into his pocket. "No," the man said. "This one's on me. Those bastards made me part of their horse stealin'. I hope you get them."

"Much obliged," Fargo said. "I'll get 'em." He swung onto the bay, took the horse onto the dusty roadway outside the shop, and set off after the hoof prints that stayed nice and clear in soft dirt. His eyes flicked to the sky. Another hour or so of daylight left. Enough, he grunted silently. The three men had ridden at an easy canter, it appeared, pulling the Ovaro behind them. They probably felt secure, stayed on the road a good while before finally turning off into hill country. The old bay moved well enough, Fargo noted, but, bending low in the saddle, he heard the slight rasp deep in the horse's chest and forced himself not to push the animal too hard. He was gaining, anyway, their prints getting fresher as they slowed going up into the hills. Fargo rode steadily after the trio as he cursed each minute that ticked away. Nellie Noonan's life ebbed away with every goddamn tick, he thought. When he reached a hill-country plain, he pushed the old bay harder as the night began to lower. The bastards couldn't be far ahead now, and he was closing fast when the darkness wrapped itself around the land.

He halted, listened, heard the sounds of horses moving through thick brush, and spurred the bay forward slowly, following his ears. He halted as he heard the noises stop, then caught the distant sound of one of their horses blowing air. He dismounted, moved forward on foot, leading the bay behind him. He heard a man's cough, harsh, heavy, the cough of a man with bad lungs. Fargo tethered the bay at the end of a low branch and went forward on steps, silent as any mountain cat. The man coughed again, the sound close now. Fargo moved through trees, came in sight of the three figures, one starting a small campfire, the other two nearby.

Fargo backed away, retraced steps, almost to where he'd left the old bay. He pulled a straight, fresh branch down, broke it off, hefted it in one hand, and then drew the double-edged throwing knife from the sheath around his calf. He quickly began to whittle until he had one end of the branch fashioned into a long point. He stood up, tested the branch again, only now it was a crude but effective lance that he weighed in his hand, balanced, let fly for a half-dozen feet. Retrieving the branch, he crept forward again, moved silently through the trees to where they had gotten the small fire started. One man sat in front of the fire with a forked branch, heating strips of beef. Fargo's eyes went to the other two. The one with the tan vest held the big Colt .45 in his hands, examining the gun.

"Jesus, this is a nice piece," Fargo heard him say.

The other one coughed his answer. "We sell it, split the money," he managed between bursts of coughing. Fargo moved sideways through the trees, a small circle as, eyes narrowed, he measured space, distance, counted off seconds. The three rotten bastards had already jeopardized Nellie Noonan's life by hours. There was time only to strike swiftly, viciously, each move calculated with deadly accuracy. He circled a half-dozen feet to his left again. He was directly in back of the one at the fire. The short one still admiring the big Colt sat not more than six feet away and the cougher leaned against a tree a few yards on, confidently relaxed.

Fargo's glanced swept the scene once more, a final measurement. He rose, the lance he had fashioned in his left hand, the double-edged throwing knife in his right. He flung the knife first, sending the blade hurtling through the night. "Don't see why I can't keep this piece," the one with the tan vest said as he held the Colt. His answer came wrapped in cold steel that hurtled into the left side of his neck and came partly out the right side. Fargo didn't wait to see him drop the Colt, grab at his neck with both hands as a torrent of red cascaded from his mouth. The Trailsman was already running, powerful leg muscles driving him across the ground. He slammed into the figure at the fire with the force of a stampeding buffalo and the man catapulted forward into the fire, his face smashing into the flaming pieces of wood. His scream split the night but Fargo was leaping, diving over the fire, executing a somersault to land on his back on the other side. He was rolling into the brush as the third man got his first shot off, followed with two more wild shots.

Fargo, in the brush, glimpsed the other man rolling on the ground, screaming in anguish as little pieces of flame danced over his face. Fargo rolled again, deeper into the brush, heard two more shots explode. They were closer, whistling over his head, and he ducked around the trunk of a hackberry. He shifted the makeshift lance to his right hand, crouched as the third man came toward him, gun in his hand, peering into the darkness. His arm was drawn back when he straightened, hurled the crude lance at his target, and dropped to the ground at once. The man spun, fired at the sound. The lance struck him alongside the temple as he twisted away, yet with enough force to send him sprawling backward. Fargo darted forward as the man landed on his back, scooped up the length of branch, and drove forward with it. The man started to bring his gun up as Fargo drove the lance into his solar plexus, all his strength and weight behind it. The crude point made a jagged tear of a hole as it plunged into the man, rupturing innards, tearing aside tissue. The man emitted a deep gurgling sound as his torso jerked convulsively. Fargo stepped back, left the crude lance in place, shaking violently as the man's body jerked in its convulsive death throes.

He turned away, took two steps, and emerged from the brush to retrieve his gun. It lay beside the still figure that continued to spill red from its gaping mouth. He bent over, yanked his throwing knife free, cleaned the blade on the grass, and put it away. He was swinging onto the Ovaro when he cast a glance at the third figure lying to one side—long, low, moans emanating from what had once been a face but seemed now to be only a charred, still-smoking side of meat. Fargo wheeled the Ovaro in a tight circle and headed from the scene, anxious only to make up time. They had taken almost three hours from him, and from Nellie Noonan, and he cursed their rotten hearts as he rode on. The night was deep when he finally halted. A tired horse could still make time, an exhausted one was certain trouble. He unsaddled the Ovaro and stretched himself out on a soft bed of elf's-cap moss, let his tired body ease itself into relaxed calm. Once again, he went over the beginnings of it, the little town of Flatwheel and the saloon in the center of main street.

He'd stopped in at the saloon to see Charley Oxman. Charley had been bartending there for almost two years, since he had his leg broken in three places by a steer. His steer-wrestling days over, he'd turned to tending bar and they had talked about old days and old ways. Fargo remembered how he had a shot glass of bourbon almost to his lips when he heard the man's voice carry through the hum of conversation. He'd frozen in place, fingers curling tight around the shot glass.

"First woman they ever hung in Brushville," the man's voice had said. "Nellie Noonan's her name."

Fargo had almost shattered the shot glass in his hand, lowered it to the bar, and turned, his eyes boring into the man, a thin-faced, slight-built, balding man wearing a waistcoat and fancy suspenders, talking to a bearded companion. "Say that again, mister," Fargo growled. "About Nellie Noonan."

The slight-built man turned, leveled a glance of mild curiosity at him. "I said they're going to hang her," he repeated.

Fargo had snapped out steel-muscled arms, seized the man by the shirtfront, and lifted him from the ground as though he were a child. "You talking big, telling stories, mister?" he rasped. "You lying, spreading rumors?"

The man's eyes filled with fear and awe as his feet dangled in the air. "No, Jesus, no stories," he said. "I just left Brushville a few days back. I wouldn't make up somethin' like that."

Fargo forced his hands to unclasp and he lowered the man to the ground, saw the man swallow hard and relief come into his fear-filled eyes. "Jesus, mister, you got an interest or somethin'?"

"Nellie Noonan," Fargo frowled. "Nellie's no candidate for hanging. Never could be, not Nellie. Something's wrong, some kind of mistake. Tell me more."

The man shrugged. "They say she shot and killed Judge Counsil," he said.

"Nellie Noonan? Never, not her. There's something wrong," Fargo snapped back.

"They say she still had the gun in her hand when they reached the judge," the man answered. "Judge Counsil was a powerful man in Brushville, nobody you go around shooting."

"It's a lie, a goddamn lie," Fargo flung back. "I know Nellie Noonan. She wouldn't shoot a soul."

The man shrugged again. "Heard she'd been having an affair with the judge and tried to push

him for more money. He said no, walked out on
her, and she up and shot him."

"Never," Fargo roared. "That's either the big-
gest damn mistake anybody ever made or it's a
pack of goddamn lies."

The man swallowed hard again. "Don't get mad
at me, mister. All I know is what I heard. They're
going to hang her Thursday," he said.

"Thursday?" Fargo remembered exploding.
"Shit, that's only two days from now." He'd spun
on his heel and raced out of the saloon, leaving a
torrent of oaths behind him. Two days. Not enough
time, he'd swore as he vaulted onto the Ovaro
hitched outside. Not enough time, but he had to
somehow make it enough. He'd raced from the
town, crossed the Salmon River, and galloped
north and west. He'd made good time until the
horse cracked the hoof and he wound up in the
smithy's. The rest needed no reliving, three hours
spent, three hours that belonged to Nellie Noonan.
He cursed softly, put his arms behind his head,
and old memories swam into his mind. Nellie
Noonan had always been one of the good people
in this world, pretty and sweet and quick with a
smile. But it was so much more than that. Nellie
was one of the caring people, one of those few
who put the needs of others before their own
needs.

Nellie Noonan a killer? Fargo gave a harsh, wry
snort. Never, not Nellie. He hadn't seen her in
three years but that made no difference. He knew
Nellie Noonan, knew what she could do, but more
important, what she couldn't do. Something was
wrong. Something stunk like a carp in the sun
for three days, he muttered. He closed his eyes,

forced sleep on himself, and was in the saddle again at dawn. He crossed to the edge of the Bitterroot Range where a good trail let him make time, the ground kept smoothed by the trappers and their pack mules and the fur traders who drove their wagons as far north as Payette Lake.

Brushville lay just west of the Bitterroot and he held to a steady pace, reined up only when he caught sight of the five near-naked horsemen on a distant ridge. He squinted in the morning sun but they were too far away to pick out markings. The northern Shoshone rode this land, as did the Nez Percé, and the Kiowa came over the Montana border all too often. He hung back, anxious only to avoid further delays, until they disappeared down the other side of the ridge. When they were out of sight he spurred the pinto forward, continued on with a steady pace. Three hours were proving damned hard to make up and he pushed the pinto until night fell once more and he bedded down, gave the horse and himself as much rest as he dared. He was in the saddle again as dawn painted its pink edges along the mountaintops.

It was Thursday, dammit, he swore through tightened lips, and he'd still a good way to go to reach Brushville. He bent low in the saddle, cutting down wind resistance as the Ovaro's gleaming black fore- and hindquarters and pure white midsection glistened in the sun. He watched the golden sphere climb into the noon sky and the dryness in his mouth grew bitter. He flung an oath into the hot, dry wind and listened to the steady drumbeat of the pinto's hooves. Fields of lavender-blue chickory blossomed on his left and on the right, bright pink rockrose made the high banks shimmer with beauty. Damn, it was a day for life and beauty, he swore, not a day for hanging. And surely not Nellie Noonan's hanging. He'd stopped watching the sun move across the afternoon sky when Brushville came into sight, nestled at the foothills of the Bitterroot Range, a town that had set itself at the start of the north passage into Washington State and became the jumping-off place for every wagon train and sodbuster headed to the far West.

Brushville had sprouted with the traffic, had stores and a proper bank where settlers could get cash for supplies and a fancy house separate from the saloon. Nellie had opened a piece-goods store when he last saw her and was happy and well. The flash of remembering brought a grimness to his mouth and he spurred the pinto full out for the last few hundred yards, slowed only when he reached town.

The wide main street had the usual collection of wagons and horses tied to hitching posts. Fargo's eyes swept down the dirt street, across the figures moving back and forth. No crowd gathering, he grunted, no loungers waiting alongside the wooden buildings. He wanted to seize hope but could feel only a grim apprehension. He reined up outside a window with gold letters painted onto the glass: SHERIFF'S OFFICE—R. COLEMAN. He swung down from the pinto and walked through the open door. A man looked up from a battered desk in the front room, beefy-faced, with gray, wary eyes, a frame too thick around the middle but with shoulders still bearlike.

"You the sheriff?" Fargo bit out and the tension was in his voice and in the ice blue of his eyes.

"That's right." The man nodded. "Rob Coleman."

"Heard you had a hanging set for today."

The man nodded again. "You come to watch?"

"I came to stop it." Fargo saw the gray, wary eyes grow more wary, narrow a fraction as the man took in his big, powerfully muscled frame, the intenseness of his chiseled features.

"Either way, you're too late," Sheriff Coleman said. "We did it yesterday, change in plans."

Fargo's words came from his lips with ominous slowness. "You hung Nellie Noonan yesterday," he repeated.

Sheriff Coleman felt a stab of uncomfortableness as the big man's eyes speared into him as though he were a fly on a pin. "That's right," he said. "Sorry."

"Not near as sorry as you're going to be," Fargo said, and his words were sheathed in ice.

Exciting Westerns by Jon Sharpe from SIGNET

(0451)

☐ **THE TRAILSMAN #1: SEVEN WAGONS WEST**
(127293—$2.50)*
☐ **THE TRAILSMAN #2: THE HANGING TRAIL** (110536—$2.25)
☐ **THE TRAILSMAN #3: MOUNTAIN MAN KILL** (121007—$2.50)*
☐ **THE TRAILSMAN #4: THE SUNDOWN SEARCHERS**
(122003—$2.50)*
☐ **THE TRAILSMAN #5: THE RIVER RAIDERS** (127188—$2.50)*
☐ **THE TRAILSMAN #6: DAKOTA WILD** (119886—$2.50)*
☐ **THE TRAILSMAN #7: WOLF COUNTRY** (099052—$2.25)*
☐ **THE TRAILSMAN #8: SIX-GUN DRIVE** (121724—$2.50)*
☐ **THE TRAILSMAN #9: DEAD MAN'S SADDLE** (112806—$2.25)*
☐ **THE TRAILSMAN #10: SLAVE HUNTER** (114655—$2.25)
☐ **THE TRAILSMAN #11: MONTANA MAIDEN** (116321—$2.25)
☐ **THE TRAILSMAN #12: CONDOR PASS** (118375—$2.50)*

*Prices slightly higher in Canada

**Buy them at your local
bookstore or use coupon
on next page for ordering.**

SIGNET Westerns You'll Enjoy

(0451)

- [ ] **CIMARRON #1: CIMARRON AND THE HANGING JUDGE by Leo P. Kelley.** (120582—$2.50)*
- [ ] **CIMARRON #2: CIMARRON RIDES THE OUTLAW TRAIL by Leo P. Kelley.** (120590—$2.50)*
- [ ] **CIMARRON #3: CIMARRON AND THE BORDER BANDITS by Leo P. Kelley.** (122518—$2.50)*
- [ ] **CIMARRON #4: CIMARRON IN THE CHEROKEE STRIP by Leo P. Kelley.** (123441—$2.50)*
- [ ] **CIMARRON #5: CIMARRON AND THE ELK SOLDIERS by Leo P. Kelley.** (124898—$2.50)*
- [ ] **CIMARRON #6: CIMARRON AND THE BOUNTY HUNTERS by Leo P. Kelley.** (125703—$2.50)*
- [ ] **LUKE SUTTON: OUTLAW by Leo P. Kelley.** (115228—$1.95)*
- [ ] **LUKE SUTTON: GUNFIGHTER by Leo P. Kelley.** (122836—$2.25)*
- [ ] **LUKE SUTTON: INDIAN FIGHTER by Leo P. Kelley.** (124553—$2.25)*
- [ ] **COLD RIVER by William Judson.** (098439—$1.95)*
- [ ] **DEATHTRAP ON THE PLATTER by Cliff Farrell.** (099060—$1.95)*
- [ ] **GUNS ALONG THE BRAZOS by Day Keene.** (096169—$1.75)*
- [ ] **LOBO GRAY by L. L. Foreman.** (096770—$1.75)*
- [ ] **THE HALF-BREED by Mick Clumpner.** (112814—$1.95)*
- [ ] **MASSACRE AT THE GORGE by Mick Clumpner.** (117433—$1.95)*

*Prices slightly higher in Canada